"The author captures the raw emotions of this family as it experiences years of dysfunction. Their path thru life is filled with tragedy after tragedy, and you feel their pain as you root for wholeness and well being to take center stage. New author Kenya Spear craftily spins a tale of family turmoil enriched with brutal honesty, that captures the reader's heart from the very first page."

Sibyl Renae Kerr, Playwright and Producer

"In her debut novel Kenya Spear manages to get thru to the heart of a family's complex relationships. In language both spare and poetic, she delves into the heartbreak, the betrayals, and the nightmare specter of dreams deferred that hangs over all. Yet the family each in their own way wages a valiant struggle to come to terms with their private demons and recognize that the human spirit is much stronger than they imagined".

Grace Edwards, Author of The Viaduct, The Mali Anderson Mysteries, and In the Shadow of the Peacock

"First time author Kenya Spear provides a compelling story full of intrigue, courage and strength of a child who rises above the dysfunctional behavior of his family. Each character is thoroughly presented which makes you feel as though you know each one of them personally. This makes for a very good read."

Rodney J. Reynolds, American Legacy Magazine

FURIOUS RED

Kenya Spear

iUniverse, Inc.
New York Bloomington

Furious Red

iUniverse books may be ordered through booksellers or by contacting:

iUniverse
1663 Liberty Drive
Bloomington, IN 47403
www.iuniverse.com
1-800-Authors (1-800-288-4677)

ISBN: 978-0-595-51795-4 (pbk)
ISBN: 978-0-595-62036-4 (ebk)

Printed in the United States of America

iUniverse rev. date: 5/21/2009

To the memory of my paternal aunts, Marie Shelton Thomas, Dinah Mae Shelton, and Alberta Shelton Mobley; my paternal uncle, James "Jimmy" Shelton; my maternal aunts, Emma, Marie, Artie, Thelma Lou, Frances, and her husband, Arthur; and Aunt Geraldine Smith Pryor and her daughters, Linda and Clare Jane. I never forgot any of you, and I never will.

Acknowledgments

The completion of this book is the result of my pursuit of a dream. It is overwhelming to realize that my vision has finally been achieved. I would like to express my appreciation to the following people who helped me along the way.

Elaine G. Ruskin witnessed the beginning. Teresa E. Warren heard the pieces. Mary Joseph Barnes who is a friend, and Zaline Marie Scott-McShan (1956-1998) who was a friend. And my husband, Samuel L. Spear Jr., is and was always supportive and loving. I could not have done it without you, Sam!

Wilt thou be angry with us forever? Wilt thou
draw out thine anger to all generations?
Psalm 85:5, KJV

Prologue

When I was eight years old in 1953, I created a character called Furious Red. I wrote stories and drew pictures of him. Like me, Furious Red was tall and thin with skin as dark as black coffee. He lived in the projects and rode a yellow bus to school each day. I filled my notebook with stories about his dreams of leaving the projects, owning a red Ford convertible, and perhaps traveling to Hawaii some day.

I showed my crammed notebook to my teacher, Miss Griffin, who flipped through the pages and smiled.

"May I take this home?" she asked.

The next day, she pulled me aside and said, "Buddy, your pictures and the language of Furious Red are very good. You have a wonderful imagination."

"I want to be a writer," I said proudly.

"You have skill," Miss Griffin said, "but you need to pay closer attention to your spelling. Use a dictionary to look up words before writing them down."

"Yes, Miss Griffin," I replied and beamed with pride.

"You remind me of Langston Hughes," she added.

"Who?"

"Langston Hughes. He is probably the greatest poet and writer alive."

"Is he really alive?"

"Yes. He travels widely, reading his work to people all over the country. He has an apartment on 127th Street in Harlem."

"He lives in Harlem? Is he a colored man?"

"Yes, he is."

Miss Griffin scanned her roll book and said, "I see you live on Sutter Avenue in Brooklyn."

"Yes, I recently moved there with my mother, sister, and baby brother."

"A library is down the block from you. Why don't you get a library card? It won't cost anything. You only need to show identification. I bet your school lunch card would do. Then you can borrow books and read about Langston Hughes and other authors, too. The library is a safe place for you. If you want to be a good writer, you need to read."

I smiled. I was going to be a writer and a good one.

Chapter One
March 1964

I dreamed of becoming a writer, and I wrote daily. One month after my nineteenth birthday, I shared my aspiration with Mom, but I wasn't prepared for her reaction.

I had come home after spending the afternoon in the library. I found Mom sitting at the kitchen table. She was smoking and drinking black coffee. She had just gotten in from her job as a housekeeper at Kings County, a large municipal hospital. The hand holding the cigarette was calloused. Her red nail polish was old and chipped. Her wrinkled, gray uniform hung on her thin, frame. Her thick, short hair was still encased in the hairnet housekeepers were required to wear at work.

"Where you been?" she asked, ignoring the load of books in my arms.

"Is that a rhetorical question?" I replied.

"Buddy! Whaddayou mean?"

"Nothing."

I wearily placed the stack on the table next to the overflowing ashtray and sat down. Her gaze darted from me to the books.

"Well, I can see you ain't been working! You ain't been at that job down at the supermarket."

"Mom, I can't work and go to school, too. I'm going to be a senior in September. I need to keep my grades up. I need an academic diploma, not a general one, if I want to attend college."

Her haggard face turned dark with anger. "I've been feeding you and keeping a roof over your head. You turned down a $1.25 an hour part-time cashier job!"

1

I was too shocked by her words to respond.

"You could be bringing in some money to help out. Your sister went to school and worked, too. So why can't you? Things ain't easy, you know!"

Living had been hard. The spring I turned eight, my sister Cleo was eleven, and our brother Timothy was just a toddler, Daddy had died, and we were evicted from the farm Down South. Social Services had given us a choice, New York City or Chicago, along with three one-way tickets on the Greyhound bus. They also gave us a letter for the welfare office, directions about riding the subway to get there, and a twenty-dollar bill for lunch money. We lived in a run-down hotel in Times Square all spring and summer and we started receiving welfare checks.

Eventually, Social Services located an apartment for us in the Van Dyke housing projects on Sutter Avenue in Brownsville, Brooklyn, one of the most depressing and crime-ridden neighborhoods in the city. Cleo and I entered school in September. Social Services helped Mom enroll Timothy in a day care center, and they found her a job in the housekeeping department at Kings County. But she managed money poorly, drank excessively, and hung out with men. She was seldom around to care for us.

I stared at her and thought, "If you didn't spend so much money on liquor, cigarettes, and your male friends, we could make it."

Mom took a sip of coffee. "I'm having it tough. I've got sickly Timothy to worry about. I've got to feed him and put clothes on his back!"

I looked away, but I wanted to say, "Mothers I know feed and clothe their children."

She smashed her cigarette out and said, "Cleo use to give one hundred dollars a month to help with this house. Now she gives less than fifty. She's spending money on records and clothes."

I thought, "Cleo is entitled to spend her money on herself."

Listening to Mom made me angry. I thought, "Why couldn't

she make an effort to budget and be a mother to us? Now she wanted me to work so I could give her money, too."

"Mom," I said slowly, "I'll think about taking the job."

Her dark eyes examined me. "Well, you over sixteen. You don't need no working papers. You should take it!"

When Cleo turned sixteen, she had obtained working papers. She was a part-time cashier in a supermarket while she juggled school, pulled meals together, and cleaned our apartment. I helped with the laundry and got Timothy ready for school.

When Cleo graduated from high school, she had gotten an office job. The manager of the supermarket, Mr. Rosenberg, who knew me well, offered her old job to me. But I had difficulties in school. I struggled to learn how to read, and I had even repeated a couple grades. I would be twenty years old and a senior in high school. I needed to concentrate on my schoolwork. I wanted an academic diploma. To Mom's dismay, I declined Mr. Rosenberg's offer.

"I need more time to think about it," I said, frustrated.

"You always thought you were so special." Mom reached over and emptied her cup into the sink.

I started to walk toward the bedroom I shared with Timothy. "I want to be somebody. I want to go places and do things. I don't want to spend the rest of my life living in the projects."

Mom lit a cigarette. The smoke curled toward the window, where pink and white plastic curtains hung.

"Hmm! Go places and do things and be somebody? Whaddayou want to do and be?"

I swallowed. "I'm going to be a writer."

Mom's eyes opened wide in surprise. "Shut your mouth! A writer! Buddy, you can barely spell!"

*   *   *

One year later, I thought I was hot stuff. I was a senior in high school and I had spoken with a counselor about attending college. To smooth feelings between Mom and me, I took the part-time job at the supermarket and regularly gave her money.

But I found time to write more Furious Red stories. When doubts or depressing thoughts crossed my mind, I thought of Langston Hughes and his poem "To Be Somebody."

Oh! Little boy dreaming of the boxing gloves Joe Louis wore, the gloves that sent two dozen men to the floor. Knockout! Bam! Bop! Mop! There's always room they say at the top.

I was over six feet tall and reedy but I wasn't athletic. I couldn't sing, and my dance steps were barely adequate. But I was an avid reader. And I wrote for the *Jefferson Front*, my high school paper. I was the only Negro on the newspaper staff, and I worked hard on my stories. But I still had trouble with spelling.

Seniors took courses in life skills. We learned family planning, hygiene, and money management. Each week, we read the Civil Service newspapers and learned how to apply for federal, state, and city jobs. The salaries were decent, and the benefits were good. I wanted some of that, but I wasn't going to give up writing.

Cleo and her best friend Rita Ann had graduated from high school and started working in offices. They weren't taking care of white children or working in their mother's kitchen.

They carried Charlie spray cologne, orange lipstick, and nut-brown powder compact in their purses. They wore thread-thin gold bracelets, and their nails were neat and trimmed.

I liked Rita Ann. She was the color of a walnut. She wore her brown hair in a ponytail. She had thin lips and solid, bold legs that reminded me of the old oak tree that shaded the backyard of the house I lived in Down South. She wasn't fashionable; everything she wore looked drab on her narrow hips. But she was attractive, honest, and dependable. She was also a good cook. She made some mean fried chicken, potato salad, and corn bread.

But she scared me. I never saw her reading anything. And she had no sharp opinions or views. When conversations arose, her input was limited to saying, "That's nice," "It's okay," "For real," or "I think so, too."

I knew she was into me. She had hinted we should go out. But when I looked behind her brown cat's-eye frame glasses and into her eyes, I saw Friday night fish dinners, car notes, nine-to-five jobs, crying babies, and Sunday nights watching Ed Sullivan.

By contrast, Cleo was tall and skinny. The color of a bright yellow squash, she had long, reddish hair that hung frizzy and wild around a slender face and narrow shoulders. She was matchless. In August 1963, she had gone on the March on Washington with Roy Inn's and the Congress of Racial Equality. She often wore her black-and-white CORE Freedom Now button. She played the protest songs of Odetta, Richie Haven, Joan Baez, Bob Dylan, and Peter, Paul, and Mary so loudly that I couldn't write when I wanted to. She had recently developed a love for jazz, and she had started spending her receptionist's salary on albums. The covers were posted on her bedroom walls. Jimmy Smith's *Walk on the Wild Side*, Herbie Mann's *Live at the Village Gate*, and Lee Morgan's *The Sidewinder* were some of her favorites.

After work and on weekends, she dressed in black dresses, low-heeled black boots, black leotards, and a black beret and went clubbing in Greenwich Village. She started smoking cigarettes and wearing dark glasses even when there was no sun.

"That's in," she would say.

One Friday night, she met Michael, a blond-haired, blue-eyed guy from Scarsdale who drove a sports car. He had driven down to meet friends, drink beer, and hang out in jazz clubs. He was thirty-two and a broker in his father's real estate office. He traveled to Europe each summer.

"I'm going to Europe with Michael, Buddy," she suddenly said to me one Saturday night when we were relaxing at home.

I gave her a wary look. "Cleo, I think you're flipped. You don't make enough money to buy a plane ticket."

"Who said I was going to buy the ticket?"

I gazed at the attractive woman sitting before me, a woman who had jazz facts at the tip of her tongue. She could quote jazz musicians' dates and places of birth. When listening to jazz, she could also name what instruments she heard and who was playing it. I found it remarkable how she cherished and treasured musicians' styles and flair, despite the fact that Charlie Parker was a drug addict, Dinah Washington was enormously fat, and many of the others abused alcohol and neglected their families. Oftentimes, they were womanizers who lived on the edge. This didn't affect her love for them or their music.

"Oh, you think Mr. Scarsdale is going to pay your way? He's probably just a white boy who wants to walk on the wild side with a Negro woman that's not too black."

She shook her head. Her thick hair covered her face. "Michael isn't like that."

My sister was popular, good-looking, and smart. Guys were always trying to talk to her. The thought of some suburban white dude who drove a sports car and might jerk her around got me mad as hell. I didn't respond.

"Interracial relationships are in."

"Things ain't changed that much," I retorted.

She gazed at me. "You've heard Dylan singing, 'Times They Are a-Changing'?"

"What's that got to do with Michael, Cleo?"

"He went on the March on Washington, too. His parents contribute big bucks to the NAACP."

I shrugged my shoulders.

"Michael is taking me to Europe. He's buying my ticket, but I'm saving money to spend."

I stared at her.

"I want to go where Miles Davis and John Coltrane were appreciated and treated with respect."

I took my sister's soft, slender hand.

"I think you've been influenced by the *Village Voice* and you've been listening to too much radio."

She started blushing.

"I look up to you. You read; you want to move out of the projects and travel. Girl, you motivate me, but be careful with this white man and black woman thing."

She pulled her hand away and started searching in her large bag for cigarettes.

"Remember what Dr. King said? That we cannot walk alone? We have to pledge that we'll march ahead together. Remember what he said about not being judged by the color of one's skin?"

I didn't reply. It was getting late. I needed to look at my new story and see how Furious Red was doing.

"I'm out of here," she said. She picked up her bag. "One of my favorite singers, Gloria Lynn, is opening at a club in the Village. I've got to be there."

Chapter Two
Two Weeks Later

Timothy was snoring. Mom was at work. Cleo was nowhere around. I thought about fixing a pot of coffee. When they got home, they could drink coffee, smoke cigarettes, watch TV, or read, but I was in a funk.

Last Thursday afternoon, unbeknownst to Cleo, I had boarded the A Train and got off at West 4th Street, Washington Square Park, in Greenwich Village, which is in Lower Manhattan.

I was nervous, but I wanted to see some of what she saw and often told me about. I was concerned about what to wear, so I put on black pants. My dark green turtleneck was stretched out of shape, but it worked under my jacket.

On the train, I felt shaky and questioned what I was doing. When the doors opened at West 4th Street, I thought about boarding the next train back to Brooklyn. But I saw a couple dudes walking up the steps to the street, so I followed, but I started feeling worried when I suddenly realized I had traveled a long way from the projects.

On the streets in Greenwich Village, there must have been hundreds of folks. I got caught up and started walking with them. I had very little money, knew no one, and had no idea where I was going.

But the March day was kind. Spring was nibbling, and I was soon walking toward a large arch. I walked faster because it reminded me of the arch in Brooklyn at Grand Army Plaza near the huge library where Mrs. Weisman, my sixth-grade teacher, had often taken the class. This arch was an entrance to a park.

Straight ahead was a fountain. Several white kids were running around, and colored ladies were pushing strollers.

As I walked, I noticed most women looked chic in leather pants or flowing skirts. The men with beards, goatees, and shoulder bags appeared hip and cool. When Cleo came here, she usually dressed in black, and her long hair hung loose under a beret that expressed her cockiness. I wished I looked more stylish.

I saw several green benches. Folks were sitting, not lying, on them, so I sat, too. It was peaceful, and the cool but not uncomfortable air helped me relax. But I must have dozed off. The sound of a voice with a slight Southern accent startled me.

"Want you to have this." The man thrust a leaflet at me.

*The Progressive Black Students of New York
University Invite You to a Discussion.
"Where Is Johnson's Great Society Taking Blacks?"
Join Us Saturday, March 22, 1965, from 1:00 to 4:00 PM
For Additional Information, Call CH-6-1965*

I looked up and saw the smiling face of a short, almost fat man. He looked to be about my age. Tiny, steel frame glasses shaped like hexagons were perched on his nose.

"Earl Ernest Johnson," he said abruptly and held out his hand.

"Benson Lee Powell Jr. But everybody calls me Buddy," I said, grasping the stranger's rough, ashy hand.

"Mind if I sit?"

Before I could respond, he had dropped his knapsack, which was crammed with flyers, books, and a large bag of peanuts, and sat down. He wore a dark brown leather vest, blue jeans, and worn brogans. His white shirt was open at the neck, and his sleeves were rolled up to reveal fleshy arms. His hair was amazing. It looked like organized steel wool. His teeth were white and straight. His breath smelled of peppermint.

"I never saw you before. You part time? What's your major?"

His high-speed, self-assured voice was a clear tenor. I liked him immediately.

"Me? No, no. I'm not a student here."

"I'm a sophomore," he said, "and I pretty much know all the brothers."

I thought, "He said brothers like it was a proper noun."

"And those I don't know, I want to know. That's why I woke you up to give you the flyer." He looked me in the eyes as he spoke.

I glanced down at the yellow paper again and back at Earl Ernest, who was still watching me intently.

"You live Uptown? How often you come down here?"

"I live in Brooklyn. This is my first visit to the Village."

"Brooklyn? I've never been there. I'm from Laurel, Virginia, a small town. I'm on scholarship. I was going to attend Virginia Union. My parents graduated from there. It's about twenty-five miles from our house, but NYU offered a generous package. These white colleges want a few of us now, so here I am. I'm a political science major. I'm going to be a lawyer."

"I'm a senior at Thomas Jefferson High School," I said. "I've been thinking about college, and I've got some other things going on, too."

"So why don't you come on down here and check it out on the twenty-second." He pointed to the flyer.

"I don't know. I'm working then." I was starting to feel awkward. He seemed so together.

"Well, think about it." He rose to leave. "Hold tight to the flyer. You can leave a message for me at that number." He tapped his bag. "Got to get rid of these."

I watched him walk toward the arch. He wobbled like an overweight duck. The cumbersome shoulder bag caused him to lean a little to the left. I watched until he was out of sight. I looked at the flyer again.

"Society … blacks."

I started to recall my earliest awareness of the image of blacks in society.

I had read about Dick, Jane, Spot, dumpy grandmother, smiling grandfather, stay-at-home mother, and tall, skinny, briefcase-carrying father, but something was missing. However, probing through the shelves at the library, I found *A Treasury of Stephen Foster*, a book of music. Songs like "Uncle Ned," "Old Black Joe," and "Nelly Bly" were all illustrated in pen, colored pencils, and inks. I scanned the pages. I thought of my illustrations of my Furious Red stories, but this was different. I saw sketches of fancy white women and gentlemen and well-dressed children with family pets. I also saw people who looked like me. I saw old men humped over with hats in hands. Shoeless women in head rags and tattered dresses were sweeping dirt floors with makeshift straw brooms. I saw barefoot children, girls with unkempt hair and falling hem dresses, and boys whose shirttails hung out of patched trousers. I was a child then. It made me feel so good to see black people in a book. But I later realized the portrayal of my people had been callous, cruel, coldhearted, and degrading.

Thinking of Stephen Foster's portrayals depressed me. I often felt deprived. I was born to poor, needy people who were barely getting by. I was ashamed and embarrassed. I was determined to be different. I would develop myself as an artist. I would read and see all I could and then write about it. I knew I would be somebody.

A barking dog brought me back to the present. I wanted to be a writer, but could I do it? What would I do until I was able to support myself as a writer? What could I do? How was I to live? Could I continue to live with Mom, Cleo, and Timothy? Several seniors in my high school had taken Civil Service exams. Bernard, a friend since third grade, was engaged. But I never gave serious thought to marriage or children. Those ideas remained in the back of my mind.

I thought long and hard about my attributes. I was respectful. I looked at people when I spoke to them. I believed in God. I didn't smoke or steal. I helped around the house. I carried shopping bags for old ladies. I spent time with Timothy. I had Cleo's back, but I didn't know who had mine.

I stuffed Earl Ernest's flyer into my tattered jacket pocket and walked slowly back to the subway. When I arrived home, I heard the ringing phone.

"Hello."

A white girl's voice asked, "Is Cleo there?"

"No, she's not," I said, not checking to see if Cleo was in her room. I knew that, if she were, jazz would be playing.

"Do you know when she left? Was it long ago?"

The kitchen's wall clock said ten fifteen.

"I got in a few minutes ago. She wasn't here."

"She was to meet us at the Five Spot at ten. Has she called?"

Cleo often talked about the Five Spot, a jazz club in the Village.

"No. Who's there tonight?"

"Lambert, Hendricks, and Ross."

I knew of them. They were a popular jazz vocalist group made up of one white man, one black man, and one white woman. Cleo played their albums often.

"Maybe she got stuck on the train. Give her a few minutes. If she calls, what should I tell her?"

"Jill and Michael are waiting inside. Michael has paid the cover charge. She just needs to come on in."

I hung up. In the silence, I thought about Furious Red. I needed to write. But I didn't feel like it after the phone call. I walked down the hall to see if Mom was in her bedroom. She wasn't. Timothy was sleeping soundly in the bedroom we shared. He had pulled the covers over his head. Seeing him alone in our apartment made me very angry.

I thought, "How long has he been home by himself? Did

Mom fix him something to eat and then go out? Did Cleo come home from work, feed him, and then leave to hang out with her friends?"

I wanted to believe they had, but I knew Timothy had been on his own for hours. I felt guilty about leaving our apartment before he got home. I should have waited. I would have fixed him a quick snack and asked Aunt Rosa, our next-door neighbor, if she would keep an eye on him.

I thought about waking him up to ask if he were all right and if he were hungry. But he looked so peaceful. I closed the door and went into the kitchen. I fixed coffee and left it on the stove. I went to bed and had a dream.

The principal and assistant principal's smiling faces were too good to be true. Mom, Cleo, Timothy, and Daddy (now alive) were in the audience. I was wearing a brand-new suit, the first suit I had ever owned. It was cheap, but I owned it. My shoes were shining, my hair had been neatly trimmed, and my dark blue tie was straight. When the principal called my name, I walked up the steps. I was strutting across the stage to receive my diploma. My heart was beating fast, my breath was short, and I felt good. I was the first male in the family to graduate from high school. I was the second person after Cleo.

I heard clapping. Out the corner of my eye, I saw my family standing. I extended my right hand. Just as I grabbed that piece of paper, it turned wet and hot. Water started to ooze over my fingers. It covered my hand and ran over my arm and down my leg. Timothy had peed on me. I woke up.

I reached over and shook him hard. He woke up, saw my face, and started to cry. Snot ran from his nose. He wiped it on the back of his hand. I wanted to hit him upside his peanut head. His sobs were hard and loud.

Despite his bawling, he said, "I sorry, Buddy."

I pulled him close. We sat in the urine-soaked bed, and I thought about how I had to get everything done and be at school on time on this mean Friday morning in March. I showered and rushed Timothy to take his. He was tall, and his thin body dismayed me. I could see ribs poking through his pale, yellow-brown skin. He had birdlike legs and long, narrow feet. His head sat atop a stick neck. He looked deformed.

In the kitchen, Mom's coat was tossed over the back of one of our yellow plastic chairs. I noticed a half-full pot of cold coffee and a crumbled White Castle napkin on the table near a butt-laden ashtray. Her bedroom door was closed. Still, there was no sign of Cleo.

I fixed two slices of toast and a cup of hot, sugar-laden tea for Timothy. I watched his hollow cheeks move up and down as he chewed. He sipped the tea.

"Don't burn yourself," I warned him.

He finished and put on his thin coat. I rushed him into the elevator. We walked the two short blocks to his school. Then I sprinted to get to my school on time. The March wind was kicking my butt. I hunched over and darted along, wishing I had taken the time to fix myself a cup of tea.

Now, as I reflected, I started to feel miserable and thought, "What would it take to bring my family together?"

* * *

A few days later, I heard the hard bebop sound of Clifford Brown's trumpet in the hallway. I knew Cleo was home. But the odors in the hall were unfamiliar. I wondered if they were coming from our apartment. I walked down the entry and realized they were. I heard Mom laughing, and it hit me.

Today was March 15, Mom's thirty-eighth birthday. I didn't have a card or a gift. I rushed back to catch the elevator. Perhaps the bodega across the street had birthday cards in English.

The elevator door had closed. I headed for the stairs, but I decided against it when I saw broken beer bottles on the steps. I waited anxiously for the elevator to return. I had a lot on my mind. June 23 was my graduation day. I was putting a little money aside to buy my school ring and yearbook, and I was still very concerned about Timothy. Frequently, when I came home from school, I would find him alone, watching television or sleeping. He wasn't eating right, and his asthma was acting up. He used his inhaler so frequently that it increased his restlessness and sleeplessness, and he regularly missed school.

Aunt Rosa was willing to watch out for him. She checked on him when he got home from school. She often fixed him something to eat, but she had been recently diagnosed with diabetes. I was concerned. Cleo and Mom needed to be around and involved. Lately, Cleo was spending weeknights away from home. More and more often, Mom didn't come straight home after work.

Two days before, I had spoken to Mom.

"Mom, you been hanging out?" I smiled when I said it. I wanted her to know I was concerned.

She took a drag on her cigarette. In a low voice, she said, "Yeah, me and Charles spend a lot of time together."

"Charles?" I asked, surprised.

"He works with me. He nice, too." Her dark face broke into a wide smile.

"So Mom has another new man," I thought.

I wanted to suggest she spend time with Charles here so she could take care of Timothy, fix his meals, and get him ready for school, but I said nothing.

A little later, I spoke to Cleo. "Why aren't you coming home at night?"

"After clubbing and hanging out, I don't want to take the long subway ride to Brooklyn."

"Where are you sleeping?" I asked guardedly.

"When I'm with Michael, we sleep in hotels. Other times, I crash at my friend Zelda's pad on the Upper West Side."

I shook my head. While hanging out, Cleo had met artists like dancers, actors, and actresses. She craved their arty style and their creative and imaginative way of living. She was even more committed to leaving Brooklyn and the projects. She wanted to get a place in Manhattan and go to Europe with Michael.

Mom and Cleo were at home now. This could have been a good time to talk with them again. But talking to them at Mom's birthday celebration wasn't right.

The elevator arrived. Clad in a navy blue dress, matronly looking Rita Ann stepped out.

"Buddy," she said, offering her cheek for a kiss, "Why you standing at the elevator? How come you ain't in there with the music and the partying? I can smell the food way out here!"

"Rita," I said slowly, "I forgot Mom's birthday! I don't have a card or a gift."

She frowned.

"I'm going to find a card," I whispered.

"I'll go with you."

We stepped into the elevator.

"So, Buddy, you graduating in June. Have you been looking for a job?"

I looked at Rita Ann, slowly sizing her up.

I thought, "Should I share my ambitions with her?"

I considered telling her about my plans to become a writer and attend college. But I thought it better not to say anything.

"Rita, I'm taking it day by day. How is your job?"

"It's a J-O-B. A file clerk at an insurance company." Her thick ponytail swung as she turned away from my stare.

"Well, do you think about leaving? Doing something else?"

"I don't know," she said softly.

"If you could do anything you wanted, what would you do?"

16

Her eyes examined me. She shrugged and I decided to let it go.

As I suspected, I didn't find any English language cards at the bodega. Rita Ann and I walked north toward Pitkin Avenue. Merchants had shops and newsstands there. We walked past Italian pizza parlors where the lunchtime crowd ordered the two-dollar lunch special, two slices of pizza and a small soda. We walked past the East New York Savings Bank, where a young, black female teller had recently been hired. We passed Moon Chung, supposedly the best Chinese restaurant in East New York. We passed the Loews movie theater where guys took girls on dates.

At a stationery shop, I bought a simple but elegant card with yellow, white, and pink flowers on the cover. I also purchased a box of Whitman Chocolates, which the clerk wrapped for me.

A bustling newsstand at the corner sold magazines, gum, candies, cigarettes, and newspapers.

"Rita, are you familiar with the *Chief* and the *Leader*?" I dug for change in my pocket.

She shook her head.

"Here," I said, placing the two papers I purchased in her hand.

"You might want to read them. They tell how to file for jobs for the federal, state, and city government."

"For real?" she asked.

On the side streets, we glimpsed private homes and children of recent immigrants from the West Indies and the South playing stickball and riding bicycles with children of the established Jewish and Italian homeowners.

* * *

Outside my apartment, the music had gotten louder. The aromas were stronger. I unlocked the door.

Timothy started yelling, "Buddy! Rita Ann!"

I gently tugged his ear. Cleo and Mom rushed over. I was happy to see them together. Timothy was jumping up and down with delight, and this made things special.

I glanced at the yellow, green, and red balloons taped on the ceiling, and I had to bend my head. A large cooler, overflowing with beer and soda, had been placed in a corner of the living room.

Our sofa was pushed to the wall to make space for dancing. Aunt Rosa and several neighbors sat at the dining table, where a punch bowl and platters of food caught my attention.

Mom looked different. She was beautiful. Her hair had been pressed and curled. It looked soft and easy, like it did in photos of her and Daddy. Her dress was beige and green. Pink rhinestones dotted the V-neck and cap sleeves. She wore open-toed shoes, and her toenails were polished a bright red color to match her fingernails. Radiant red lipstick accented her full lips, and she laughed and laughed. The laughter carried me back.

*   *   *

It was a hot and humid July afternoon. Daddy was preparing for his weekly trip to town.

"Senior, you take the list and go 'cause I'm going to soak in a tub of Epsom salt. Yesterday, I pulled my back out chopping," Mom said.

"Clara Mae, you don't listen. I told you to take it easy." Daddy picked up his lopsided straw hat. "I reckon I need to be on my way."

Cleo and I watched the old car kick up dust. Then we took off. Cleo wanted to visit Cousin Brenda to play with the twins.

I reluctantly decided to accompany her. The twins, Mickey and Mildred, had everything, including store-bought bread, an inside toilet, toys, and books. I didn't want to go.

"Cleo, I'll walk you. Then I'm turning around."

"Buddy, why you got to be that way? You just jealous 'cause they got things."

"I'm not!"

"Yes, too!" Cleo said emphatically.

"You play up to them. They think they hot. One day, I'm going to have stuff, but I ain't going to be no show-off."

I walked Cleo to the edge of Cousin Brenda's farm and quickly headed back home. As I got closer, I saw a black pickup truck in the yard. It belonged to Mr. Robby, the colored undertaker's helper. He was tall and peanut shell brown with close-cut hair. I liked Mr. Robby. He often came to buy eggs. Cleo and I would be playing and see his pickup truck coming down the road. From the pocket of his worn leather jacket, he pulled Mary Janes for Cleo and a Payday candy bar for me. He would sit on the front porch sipping lemonade my mother served from jelly jars while Daddy puffed on his corncob pipe.

After a while, he'd say, "Boy, get eggs."

I would hustle off. I loved selling him eggs 'cause I practiced my math.

"These here eggs are seventy-five cents a dozen, so how much is a half-dozen, boy?"

Giving the correct answer would encourage him.

"Boy, how much would three eggs be, then?"

When I answered that correctly, too, Mr. Robby would laugh his thunderous cackle and slap his tight thighs with large, hairy-knuckled hands.

"I declare! You got yourself a smart boy here," he'd say to Daddy.

My father would nod and take a puff on his pipe.

I could have burst out of my pants with pride. Now I wondered why his truck was in our yard. Daddy was gone. Mother's back was hurting. I was walking by the dining room window when I heard the voices.

"Baby, you said you'd handle him, but I wondered how."

"You don't have to worry. I gave him a good-sized list. He'll be a long while." My mother said. Her laughter was high.

"Mae," Mr. Robby said in a heavy voice, "I've been waiting so long for this. Girl, you know I been coming around buying eggs just to see you. I need to be buying silk stockings and helping you put 'em on." Mom laughed harder. "How you put up with that old man? You should be going with me on my next trip to Chicago."

Mom's laughter was higher and longer. "I would be strutting down the street in some tight number?"

"Girl, you would be looking finer than wine. I wouldn't be able to keep my hands off you."

"You talk such jive."

"Mae Baby, you're too much. Come sit on my lap."

I heard my mother's skirt rustling. I moved toward the window and stood on my tiptoes. I didn't understand what I saw, but I knew it was something I shouldn't have seen. Mom was sitting on Mr. Robby's lap. Her long, red skirt was spread over and about. Mr. Robby's right hand was frantically moving up and down under it. The rapid movement caused the material to fall and rise. The sound was like a lash to my ears. Mom's head was thrown back. Her mouth was open, and she was laughing excitedly. I watched until they started kissing, but I ran away when Mr. Robby got on his knees and put his head under Mom's garment. They never knew I had been a witness.

* * *

"Buddy," Cleo said, pulling my arm, "You all right? Let's get some food and sangria."

I looked around. Mom's party was a blast. Music was playing. Folks were laughing, eating, drinking, and having a good time.

"Sangria?"

"It's the in thing," she said. "Michael and I drink it all the time."

Cleo looked incredible. She wasn't wearing dark glasses, and her wild hair was now silky around her shoulders. She wore large hoop earrings, a small pinky ring, and thin, colorful bangles. Her black sweater appeared to be cashmere. Her black leather skirt was soft. The low-heeled black boots that hugged her calves gave the impression that she might have belonged somewhere else.

"Cleo, you look good."

"Michael is very nice to me."

She smiled and offered me a glass of sangria. I sipped and decided I liked it.

"Cleo, you got his nose open. He's laying out the bucks and taking you to Europe. Are you okay with all that?

"Stop being naïve," she hissed as she rolled her eyes. "Michael likes me, and he's showing it."

Just then, Rita Ann approached with a plate of fried chicken, potato salad, collard greens, corn bread, and macaroni and cheese.

"Girl, you know that's going straight to your hips."

Cleo smiled, nodding toward the overladen plate.

Rita looked hurt, so I interjected, "Tell me, Cleo, what new sounds have you been listening to?"

"Oh, Buddy," she said, "I met Buhaina!"

"Who?"

"Art Blakey! The drummer! He was playing at the Vanguard in the Village. Michael took me to see him, and he took photos of Buhaina and me and purchased *Indestructible*, his latest album. He even autographed the cover. Want to hear it?"

Mom appeared and tapped Cleo's shoulder. "Cleo, jazz is okay, but I want to hear Jackie Wilson's 'Lonely Teardrops.'"

She hurried over to the record player to put it on. Over Jackie's smooth voice, we chatted.

"I leave the last week in June," Cleo said excitedly. "I'm waiting for my passport."

"Passport!" Rita and I said simultaneously.

"I sent the application with my check. It takes about six weeks before everything is processed," Cleo said knowledgably.

"Check!" Rita's voice rose. "You have a checking account?"

"Why, yes," Cleo said, gazing at her incredulously.

I was thinking, "Where does one get a passport application? How much did it cost? How did she open a checking account?" But Aunt Rosa approached us with a girl who caused me to stop breathing.

"This here is Lola," Aunt Rosa said. "She my sister Louise's oldest child. She studying nursing down in Baltimore. She spending the weekend. She going tell me how to control my diabetes. I is worn out from going to the clinic. Them doctors don't know nothing! I sit and sit there all day, and then they just give me prescriptions for more insulin. I is tired."

I stared at Lola. I was speechless. She was as short as a drop. Her skin was the color of midnight, and her waist was the size of a minute. She had pulled back her long, thick hair and fastened it with a red barrette. She wasn't wearing earrings, and her diminutive ears reminded me of seashells I once found at Coney Island's beach. She wore a red checked dress and low-heeled black boots like Cleo's and I wondered if boots were the latest in fashion.

Lola smiled at Cleo and Rita Ann, but Rita Ann's eyes were like daggers.

"Hello," Lola said. Her voice was like soft rain on a summer day. "You must be Buddy. Aunt Rosa tells me you will be graduating in June."

"Yes," I managed to say, thinking how I wanted to get to know this girl.

"I'm a senior at City High. I'm in the nursing program. I attend school six weeks and study at Baltimore General Hospital for six weeks. In June, I'll take the state boards. When I pass, I'll be a licensed practical nurse."

"I like your boots," Cleo said. "Aren't they comfortable?"

"Yes, I'm on my feet a lot. I have to be comfortable, but I also want to be stylish."

She glanced up at me. My heart flipped. Out the corner of my eye, I saw Rita Ann move toward the dining table and pile a fresh plate high with fried chicken and potato salad.

"Well, I am graduating and planning on pursuing my writing," I said, staring into Lola's light brown eyes.

She smiled. Cleo quietly sipped her sangria.

Suddenly, I heard a loud knock at the door. Timothy hurried over.

"Who? Who?" he asked.

"Charles. It's Charles," a loud and heavy voice said.

Mom rushed over, pushed Timothy aside, and quickly flung the door open. In the entrance, a tall, chocolate-colored man with processed, greasy, graying hair held a large, crumbled, brown paper bag close to his heavy chest, as if it were gold. His shoulders were so wide that they appeared to touch the doorframe.

"Charles!" Mom said, squealing like a teenager. "You made it!"

She threw her arms around his thick neck. Timothy, who had been unceremoniously pushed aside, grabbed my hand and stared in bewilderment. Mom, sensing our presence, turned quickly.

"Charles, these are my sons, Benson and Timothy," she said hesitantly.

His heavy-lidded, dull brown eyes avoided mine. "Howdy," he said in a coarse voice.

I reached to shake his hand. I was surprised to find it as dry as cardboard. Timothy's hand felt moist as he squeezed mine while he gawked at Charles.

"I brought you something for your birthday," Charles said, handing Mom the bag.

She opened it quickly, pulled out a six-pack of beer, and smiled widely. The music had stopped. Everyone was looking at us standing in the hallway.

Cleo, the perfect hostess, walked over to usher us into the living room.

Mom said, "Charles, this is my daughter Cleo. Cleo, this here is my friend, Charles Wilkins."

He lowered his eyes and nodded. Cleo looked at me. In her clear, bright eyes, I saw loathing for Charles. I rushed over to the record player and put on "Yakety Yak." Dancing and laughter slowly resumed.

I watched Mom guiding Charles toward the sofa, where he then flopped down. He reminded me of an elephant, big and awkward. He sat with his legs opened wide. His checked polyester pants rode up to reveal gray socks that were too short and ashy ankles. Mom offered him a plate loaded with pig's feet, potato salad, collard greens, and corn bread, and a can of the beer he brought her as a birthday present. He placed the plate on the arm of our sofa, positioned the can of beer between his legs, and began eating greedily. He mixed potato salad and collard greens together and shoved it into his mouth. He reminded me of a dumpster. His mouth opened wide, shut, and clamped down quickly. He smacked his thick, cracked lips loudly.

I saw Lola leaving the bathroom, and I hurried over.

"Let's get some sangria," I said and guided her toward the punch bowl.

We sipped drinks and chatted about school, the latest movies, and our upcoming graduations.

"I will be the first nurse in my family," she said.

"I'm the first male in my family to graduate from high school," I said. "Can I get your number?"

"Of course."

Her self-confidence, attitude, and speech reminded me of Earl Ernest. I made a mental note to locate his flyer and give him a call.

When Little Anthony and the Imperials started singing, "Just Two Kinds of People in the World," I reached for her hand to dance, but the music suddenly stopped. Timothy was smiling as he walked to the middle of the crowded living room. His hair was brushed, and he looked cute in a bright blue sweater and black slacks.

"We here to celebrate Mom's birthday," he said. "Cleo, come on in!"

The apartment door opened. Cleo stepped in, carrying a large white-and-pink square cake, her gift to Mom. She had purchased the cake and kept it in Aunt Rosa's refrigerator. "Happy Birthday, Mom!" was written in big red letters. A small white candle was in the center. Aunt Rosa followed, carrying ice cream. Rita Ann had a large bouquet of carnations wrapped in bright green paper.

Cleo started singing "Happy Birthday," and everyone joined in. Mom had been sitting next to Charles, but, when she saw the cake and heard the singing, she jumped up and rushed toward Cleo and Timothy. Everyone cheered and offered gifts and cards. I embraced Mom and gave her the card and candy. She and I both smiled because it had been a long time since I'd seen my family happy.

I noticed Charles digging in his skimpy jacket pocket. He pulled out a cigar and lit it with a large, silver lighter that he closed with a loud snap. The cigar's terrible odor crawled and curled in the air. Aunt Rosa rushed to open a window, but I approached Charles with one of Mom's ashtrays.

"Put the cigar out," I said.

And for the first time, he looked me in the eye. It was a long, hard look, and I knew that he knew I disliked him.

Chapter Three
May

In the middle of April, Cleo packed her beloved albums, clothes, and books and moved out. I took over her bedroom.

"Where you going?"

"I'm living at my friend Zelda's place on the Upper West Side," she said.

She rarely visited. She called often, but her speech was hesitant and guarded when she knew Charles was around.

"How often does he visit?" she asked.

"He spends most of his time here," I said.

"So they're shacking up?"

"Mom likes him, Cleo."

"Well, how are things going?"

"There's something about him that's just ain't right, but he's here, and that's keeping Mom home and near Timothy."

"How is Timothy?"

"He's eating better 'cause Mom cooks for Charles."

"You spending time with him?"

"When I can. I need time to write, but Mom thinks I should do things with him."

"Older Brother, I know what you mean. Mom wanted me to baby-sit. She always asked for money. I'm glad I don't live there anymore."

"Yeah, I'm getting the hell out of here as soon as I can."

"Maybe we could hook up after you graduate?"

"It could work, Cleo."

"Charles ain't like Daddy."

And we started laughing and reminiscing about our father.

"He loved pecans. I crack up when I remember how you tried to make a pecan pie," I said, laughing.

"Yeah," Cleo said, giggling. "Me, you, and the twins gathered pecans from Cousin Brenda's yard. I hurried home to make a pie before he got back from town."

"Girl, you almost burned the house down. How old were you? Nine or ten?"

"I was ten. Daddy died the next summer. He died the year I turned eleven. You were eight."

There was a long silence.

"Cleo, I still miss him."

"Buddy, I always think about Daddy."

"I write about him. The world is going to read his story and ours."

I thought about how folks would read about an old, honest, hardworking black man who married a young, frisky woman child. I thought about how he dropped dead of a heart attack and how, two weeks after his funeral, lawyers and Social Services people came with papers, a truck, and suitcases. A fat white woman in a wrinkled, pink dress that was too tight ordered us to pack. An attorney walked around our house, looked at everything, and wrote on a legal pad. The truck driver sat on the porch and smoked as we threw our possessions in luggage that would later fall apart and would have to be held together with rope.

I gathered family photos and coins I had saved from selling eggs to Mr. Robby. I carefully wrapped the photos in brown paper bags, slipped the coins in an old sock, and placed it in one of Daddy's discarded Prince Albert tobacco cans. Then I stuffed it all in a corner of the suitcase I shared with Cleo. Mom stuffed her and Timothy's meager clothing in a valise, and we quietly left our house in New Ellenton, South Carolina.

In silence, we were driven into town and brought to stand in front of an elderly, balding, white man. The desk nameplate said "Mr. Martin, County Clerk."

Mr. Martin cleared his throat and looked at us long and hard. With compassion, he asked, "Ya'll got any place to go?"

No one knew Daddy had had a first wife and three grown children, two boys and a girl. They had suddenly appeared with a will. Daddy had married Mom, but he had never changed his will. The farm and all his worldly possessions were left to his first wife and their children. We had to leave.

* * *

Cleo's rapid speech brought me back to the present.

"I want to control my life, Buddy. I want to call my own shots. You know what I mean?"

"I do, Cleo."

"When they made us leave the farm and sent us to New York, I wondered if I'd survive."

"Girl, when we got off the Greyhound and got on the subway, I was scared. Remember how Mom kept yelling and telling us to hold on? And Timothy wouldn't stop crying!"

Cleo laughed. "I loved the subway ride. The way the train twisted and turned. The lights came off and on. The noise. The people jerking back and forth and bouncing up and down. It was like the time we went to the county fair and rode on the roller coaster."

"Mom was wearing a short, tight dress. I was ashamed," I mumbled.

"Sometimes it was hard for me, too." Cleo said softly.

The sadness in her voice stunned me. She was the one who did well in school and had made friends. I had problems. Many people teased me unmercifully about the way I spoke. I had a profound Southern accent. Classmates poked fun at my unfashionable clothing. Things started to lighten up a bit when Bernard and Raymond, two guys who lived in the projects, invited me to play stickball with them.

"I cringe when I think about how we spent the spring and summer living in that hotel in Times Square," Cleo said.

It was pretty bad. We lived in one room. Mom and Timothy slept in the bed. Management provided two cots for Cleo and me. We started getting welfare checks, and we ate franks, orange drinks, French fries, and ice cream from a place called Nedicks. Now and then, we bought Chinese takeout because we had no kitchen to cook in.

"It was awful," I said. "New York was nothing like what I had imagined. I was looking for streets paved with gold."

"I saw young girls wearing tight, short dresses, lots of makeup, and high heels," Cleo said, her voice rising.

"Yeah, I knew what was going on."

"Well, what you don't know is the times Mom ordered me to buy cigarettes and things for her from Eighth Avenue were the pits."

"What happened?"

"Men looked at me, put their hands in their pockets, jiggled coins, and smiled."

"That's messed up!"

"I had never seen an elevator. I had never been in one until we got to that hotel. I felt like I was in a vertical coffin. One time, a dog grabbed my ass. I scratched his hand and stomped his toes, but he just laughed and called me a tight-ass bitch. Said he liked 'em fast."

"Well, didn't you tell Mom?"

"When the elevator reached the first floor, I didn't get off. I pushed five and ran back to our room. Mom said, "you back so soon? Where are my cigarettes?" I tried to tell her what had happened, but she said, "Girl, stop your lies. Ain't nobody interested in you.' She said it just like that."

Cleo's sobs were loud. I wanted to crawl through the phone, take her in my arms, and rock her until she stopped.

"Give me your address! Tell me how to get there. I'm coming over right now!"

Between sobs, Cleo instructed me, "Get the train to 72nd Street. Then the local to 79th Street. Walk to 84th Street. My house number is 46. Ring the top bell that says 'Scott.' I'll come down."

I wrote down every word. I had never been to the Upper West Side, and I wanted to get there without any trouble. I had been writing when Cleo had called. Now I threw my journal and pen in my book bag. I figured the train ride to Cleo's would be long, so I could read my recent writings.

I threw on a turtleneck and decided I had better change my pants. The one pair of blue jeans I owned had been washed so often that the cuffs were frayed, but they were clean, so I put them on. I grabbed a handful of bills from my secret stash, the tobacco can that had once belonged to my father. Then I donned my old pea coat and headed for the door. Just as I reached to open it, Timothy came charging in from school.

"Hey, Buddy," he said breathlessly. "Where you going?"

I thought it best not to tell him the truth, so I said, "I'm going for a stroll." I winked.

"What? You never go out on Friday. You stay here reading and writing. Then you get up early and go to work at the supermarket."

"Well, maybe I have something important to do. Come on, Tim. I'm in a hurry. Let's knock on Aunt Rosa's door and ask her to keep you until Mom or Charles gets in."

"I don't need nobody to keep me. I ain't no baby. I'm eleven, almost twelve."

I glanced at my watch. Almost thirty minutes had gone by since I'd hung up from Cleo, and I was getting impatient.

"Look, just turn around and go to Aunt Rosa's."

And I pushed him out the door and locked it. I anxiously knocked on Aunt Rosa's door.

"Hi, tall, dark, and handsome," she said, giving me a wide, toothless smile. "Come on in and take the weight off your feet."

"I wish I could. But, Aunt Rosa, I need you to keep an eye on Timothy until Mom or Charles gets home. Mom is working the eight-to-four shift this week. She'll be coming soon." I glanced at my watch. It was three forty-five. "She should be here in less than an hour."

"Oh sure. Anything for you, good-looking. Come on in here, boy."

She gently pushed Timothy into her apartment. Timothy's mouth was poked out, and he rolled his big, brown eyes at me.

"Thank you," I said and waved good-bye.

Several kids were getting off the elevator. I rushed to catch it before the door closed.

"By the way—" Aunt Rosa yelled as I dashed away. "Lola is coming. She'll be here tomorrow afternoon."

"Good. I'll see her then."

The elevator door closed, and I quickly pushed the button. I hadn't seen Lola since Mom's birthday party. I had called her a couple times. She might have told me that she was coming the first weekend in May, but I couldn't think about that now. My mind was on Cleo and getting to her as quickly as possible. Hurrying out my building, I literally bumped into Cool, the project's sharp dresser, knocking his hat off.

"Man, I am sorry," I said.

"No problem," he said. He slapped me five when I handed him his cap. "But where you hustling off to?"

"Some stuff is going down that I've got to see about."

"You need a posse?" he quickly offered.

"No, I'm okay," I said. Then I sprinted toward the elevated train station.

I heard the rumbling of the train and pushed a dollar bill

through the window of the token booth. The sad-faced clerk slid six tokens and ten cents change toward me.

The train was crowded with noisy students, but I managed to squeeze into an empty seat. I dug into my book bag for my journal. I focused on a Furious Red story about a teacher who had taught a motherless boy how to read and then later married the boy's father. I had loosely based the story on my relationship with Miss Griffin, my third-grade teacher. She'd had the most influence on me.

The story was flowing, but it needed work. I was having difficulty with tense and spelling, but I couldn't concentrate. My mind wandered to Cleo. What she had shared left me overwhelmed, but I knew everything she said was true. I vividly recalled a fight she'd had with Mom when we were living in that hotel.

The August morning was hot. I heard noises through the open windows, and I reflected on the previous night when we had gone out. What I'd seen had been upsetting to me. Several store windows had pictures of half-naked women. Men walking by, looked, stopped and smiled. The streets were dirty. Fire engines roared by nonstop. Police sirens pierced the air, causing Timothy to cry. We ate at the same dingy, dirty place where mostly women with crying babies ate, along with a few old colored men and some drunken white men. They all appeared as down and out as we were.

This wasn't the New York I had heard about. In New Ellenton, when folks returned from visiting New York, they spoke of seeing fashionable women and men who drove fast, shiny, new cars. Most teachers in my small, backwoods school came to New York every summer.

"To take courses," they had told their students.

But I overhead Daddy telling Mom that they actually came to work as domestics. I didn't understand what he said, but, when our teachers returned in September, they shared their experiences with the students. They described buildings so tall that they appeared to touch the sky and how the Empire State Building was the tallest in New York and the world. And one teacher told us how, on July 28, 1945, a plane flew into the building and killed fourteen people.

Other teachers told of shopping and how colored ladies could try on clothing just like white women and how Negroes in New York weren't expected to say "ma'am" or "sir" when they spoke to white people. I heard stories of restaurants that served delicious and fancy foods. And I heard that Negroes had greater chances in New York and more opportunities to get ahead, get good jobs, and live in nice places. But I saw none of those things when we lived in that dreadful hotel.

On that hot August morning, Mom kept going to the bathroom. She finally shook Cleo awake.

"Get up! Get dressed. I need something from the drugstore."

"I'm tired," Cleo said as she rubbed the sleep from her eyes.

"Listen, you get off that cot right now 'fore I come over there and bust you!" Mom yelled. "I don't want to scream and wake up Timothy."

From my cot, I watched as Cleo slowly got up and sat on the side of her cot. She looked so fragile. During sleep, her long hair had come undone and now hung loose around her face. Her threadlike legs reminded me of twigs. Her feet were long and narrow. She sat yawning and rubbing her eyes.

"Take this money and head to the store!" Mom said, throwing a balled-up dollar bill at her.

Cleo was crying. "I don't like going to the store. I don't like riding the elevator. Men look at me and say things. I'm scared, Mom. Don't make me go."

"Ha," Mom said. "Girl, you don't got nothin' yet, so you got nothing to worry about. But mine is here. Late but here! And if you know what's good for you, you'll get your narrow ass up and out to the drugstore now!"

The train suddenly jerked, bringing me back to the present. I glanced at my watch. It was five o'clock. The train picked up speed, and I tried to relax. But it twisted, turned, roared, and went faster. I wondered if it were out of control. The lights flashed off and on. Hot air steamed through the open windows. I sat sweating and clutching my book bag to my chest, thinking this may very well be my last subway ride.

Other passengers seemed unconcerned. Two women sitting across from me were smiling and chatting. And a woman to my right was reading an article in *Life* about the opening of the World's Fair. I could hear the train's brakes, and I prayed it was slowing down. When I felt it decelerating, I thanked God that he had answered my prayers.

We pulled into 34th Street at five thirty, and I wondered how much longer it would be before I saw my sister. The train took off again as if it were being chased. Street names flashed by. 50th Street. 59th Street. The numbers were increasing, so I reread Cleo's instructions and closed my journal.

At 79th Street, I ran up the stairs two at a time. It was still light out. Broadway was noisy and crowded. When I turned on 84th Street, I noticed an immediate change. There were trees and less people. The block was quieter and cleaner than Broadway had been. At Amsterdam Avenue, the noise level decreased even more. Several people were walking dogs. And from the way the dogs walked with their heads held high, I got the impression that they were special.

I walked faster and noticed the abundance of colorful potted plants in windows. I also saw closed garbage cans sitting next to brown and beige buildings. A young woman, wearing boots similar to Cleo's, strolled toward me. Her leather shoulder bag resembled Cleo's, and I realized Cleo fitted very well in this environment.

"What would I say to her?" I thought. "Her sobbing had been so hurtful."

I saw the house, ran up the steps, and listened as the bell chimed a classical tune. Through the etched glass, I saw my barefoot sister bouncing down the steps to greet me. I enclosed her in my arms and buried my face in her hair. We held each other, as if we were reuniting after a long absence, but I suddenly couldn't say the comforting words I thought I would say. I felt tears coming fast, but I knew that, if I started crying, I would never stop, so I rubbed Cleo's back and held her tighter. I finally looked at her. Her eyes were sad, but she was smiling. I saw the dimples in her thin cheeks.

"It's good to see you," I said.

"Older Brother," she said in the high, musical way she spoke when she was excited. A bit of her old self came alive. "I'm so glad you came to Manhattan to see about me."

I stared into her eyes. "Only Sister, did you think I wouldn't come?"

"Buddy, you've told me how much you dislike riding the subway."

We walked up the stairs and entered the apartment. The entrance walls were covered with photographs of a light-complexioned, shapely, shorthaired woman who appeared to be a few years older than Cleo was. There were photographs of her dancing, standing in front of microphones, and mingling with celebrities. I immediately recognized Sammy Davis Jr., but I had no idea who the other folks were.

"How can you stand riding that subway to work every day?" I asked.

Cleo took my book bag and coat and placed it in a large closet.

"I work in Midtown, and I walk to work. How do you think I stay so trim?" She spun around to show me her form.

Her black stretch pants and white, oversized boatneck sweater fit her perfectly. Her toes and fingernails were painted pink. Thin, colorful bracelets made tinkling sounds when she moved.

"Girl, you're looking good."

She smiled, guided me into the living room, gestured for me to sit, and quickly left the room. I eased down on a long, black sofa.

The *Village Voice* was spread out, and I spied an article headlined "The Radicals at NYU." I immediately thought of Earl Ernest Johnson and reminded myself to call him.

On an ancient trunk that served as a coffee table, there was a stack of playbills topped with a book entitled *Monologues for Actresses*. I glanced through, recalling how I could barely read when I was eight years old. I thanked God I had been placed in Miss Griffin's class. Previous teachers had told me I was lazy. They'd said I wasn't trying hard enough. But Miss Griffin took her time, and I started to understand that words had parts that were called letters, and, when those words were spoken together, they made sounds, which was called reading.

But I wanted to be in! I wanted to hang out with older guys like Cool and his friends, who turned their caps backwards and wore straight leg jeans that hung neatly over white high-top sneakers. They stood around smoking, crunching potato chips, gulping sodas, and trying to hit on girls like Cleo and Rita Ann. But I had no fine clothes and no money, so I took Miss Griffin's advice and went to the library. When I wasn't reading, I was thinking up stories. They packed my head. They got long and too heavy for me to bear, so I started writing them down.

Cleo brought me back to the present when she returned with glasses, a decanter of apple juice, a bowl of grapes, and breadsticks.

"Oh, that's Zelda's," she said, nodding toward the book. "She's gone for a while. She's in a road production. She's playing Ruth in *A Raisin in the Sun*."

I had never heard of *A Raisin in the Sun*, but I promised myself to find out what it was about.

"Are those photos of Zelda in the hallway?"

"Yes."

One living room wall was exposed brick; the others were off-white. At the windows, sheer drapery panels allowed sunshine in, and the room took on a soft, mysterious look. Under the window was a stereo, with books and several albums stacked alongside. Other albums by Gloria Lynn, Sarah Vann, and Carmen McRae were on a shelf. I sipped juice and popped a few grapes into my mouth.

"It's comfortable here," I remarked.

"I love it. Zelda asked me not to smoke inside. So I was smoking at the office and when I was with Michael, but then I decided to stop. It's been hard, but I haven't had a cigarette in three weeks."

"I'm proud of you," I said, thinking how different she had become in the few weeks since she left Brooklyn. She was not dressed in black from head to toe and she wasn't speaking rapidly.

"Let me show you around," she said, reaching for my hand.

Black and brown area rugs were scattered on the wood floors. Three clay pots filled with leafy green plants hung a few inches from the living room ceiling. In the bathroom, the towels, shower curtain, and rug were white. The tall, narrow window was bare, and there was no bathtub.

"This must be the tiniest bathroom in the world," I said, smiling at my sister.

Cleo smiled. "When Michael and I spend nights in hotels, I stretch out in a tub."

The miniature kitchen was also painted white. The appliances looked as if they belonged in a dollhouse. Everything was spotless. The bedroom walls were dark, almost blue-black. A platform bed covered by a crocheted spread and small pillows dominated the room. The bed's platform was painted the same color as the walls.

"When Zelda is away, I sleep in here," Cleo said. "Otherwise, I'm on the sofa."

Several baskets held socks, bags, scarves, and sweaters. In a corner, I saw more of Cleo's records and books. A large skylight illuminated the room. By the bed, a varnished drum table held a phone and a photo of Cleo like I had never seen her before. Her hair was pinned back from her face. Her ears held dangling earrings. Around her neck was a matching necklace that appeared to be diamonds. She wore a black strapless dress that revealed narrow shoulders and sculpted arms. She looked majestic. Standing beside her was a stern-faced, clean-shaven white man wearing an expensive-looking charcoal gray suit and dark blue tie. His sky blue eyes were staring into the camera. His total appearance displayed the trappings of wealth and class.

I stared at the photo. I never thought Michael would look like the Wall Street type. I imagined him to be quirky, eccentric, or a bit odd, like I supposed Cleo to be.

"That's a serious photo of you and Michael."

"We were celebrating our six-month anniversary. He took me to dinner at the Russian Tea Room."

"You look beautiful, Cleo."

She smiled. "I met Michael's parents that night."

"You did?" I asked in astonishment.

"Michael was hailing a cab when a man called to him."

I nodded.

"His parents had come down to see Wayne Newton. He was in concert at Carnegie Hall, which is near the Russian Tea Room."

"Did he introduce you to his parents?"

"Of course!"

"Did you speak to them?"

"Yes, I did."

"Well, what did they say?"

"His father asked if I had ever seen Wayne Newton. He said Wayne was a great singer."

"Wayne Newton? I never heard of him."

"I had no idea who he was and what he sang, but a good-sized crowd was there."

"How did Michael's parent's react when they were introduced to you?"

"We shook hands. They were cool."

"Did they seem surprised that you were a Negro?" I slowly asked.

"No, no. His mother wanted to know if I liked the food at the restaurant. They seemed like really nice folks. Michael looks a lot like his mother with his blue eyes and blond hair, but he's tall like his father. His father is good-looking, but he's balding and wears old man spectacles."

"How did Michael act? Was he uptight?"

"Michael is always together. He was smiling and holding my hand."

"Yeah? Well, how did his parents react to that?" I asked cautiously.

"He later told me that his father said I was exotic looking and his mother said I was different."

I stared at Cleo. I had heard similar words from many white teachers and classmates. They told me that I wasn't like the others. I had always asked for an explanation, but I only got bewildered and embarrassed expressions on faces that turned red as fire trucks. I recalled those photos I saw long ago in that book about Stephen Foster.

"Exotic looking! Different! Oh my God!" I thought. "Michael's parents must have been surprised when they saw that Cleo didn't resemble the stereotypical female Negro."

I suddenly felt hungry again. " Cleo, the snacks were alright, but I need some real food."

"Okay," she said.

"Let's go get something to eat." I touched her arm.

"I want to stay here and talk with you. I'll order food and have it delivered."

She headed toward the living room. I followed, but not before I gazed again at the photo of her and Michael. Cleo opened the trunk and took out a pile of menus.

"Check these out and tell me what to order."

"Surprise me, but don't order Chinese food."

Silence followed. I knew we were both revisiting the same memory.

* * *

One Sunday morning when we lived in the hotel, Mom gave Timothy a bottle and put him to bed. She gave a dollar each to Cleo and me and then told us to go play. We were excited. We had two dollars to spend.

We headed to Nedicks, and I ordered a breakfast special of toast and orange juice. I got twenty-five cents in change. But Cleo said she wanted the real special (toast, bacon, two eggs any style, and coffee), but she needed an additional fifteen cents, so I gave it to her.

She and I sat side by side, eating, laughing, and watching folks on 42nd Street. She sipped coffee and raced back and forth for free refills. It felt good being together. I'm not sure how long we sat there observing people and cracking jokes, but we saw no other children, and we had no idea where to go to play. It got boring sitting and watching people, so we returned to the hotel.

Cleo used her key to open the door. When it opened, we saw Timothy sleeping on the bed. Mr. Lee from the Chinese restaurant was sitting on a chair next to it with his pants down. Mom was on her knees in front of him with her head between his legs.

Cleo and I both looked at each other. We quietly closed and locked the door and stumbled to the elevator.

*   *   *

Cleo's voice was faint as she said, "Buddy, I don't eat Chinese food."

I reached for her, and she fell limply into my arms. I held her, and she squeezed me. We stayed close for a while.

Finally, I asked, "Do you hate Mom?"

There was a long silence.

In measured tones, Cleo said, "I don't hate her, but I am ashamed of her."

I stared at Cleo. I was thinking about Mom's many male friends. Men frequently visited our place. And I was thinking how often her behavior was upsetting. The few times she showed up at parent-teacher conferences, she was intoxicated and dressed like she was going to a nightclub. I felt so humiliated. I thought the other parents and the teachers were staring at her and me.

"Mom thinks it's her wide nose and dark skin that embarrasses me, but that's not so. She whores around," Cleo said, sobbing.

I held her tighter. We sat there for a long while. The sun disappeared. Cleo moved from my grasp and turned on a lamp.

I said, "I hoped Mom would stop drinking and sleeping around."

When we were kids, I was frequently asked why my hair was black, tight, and kinky. Many people wondered why Cleo's hair was red, soft, and fine. Some people asked why I was so dark and why Cleo looked almost white. I felt as if I were being interrogated. I didn't have any answer. I didn't understand the questions. I had never paid attention to Cleo's hair or the color of her skin. After a while, I started to examine Cleo. I noticed we really didn't favor one another, the way brothers and sisters usually did. I wanted to ask why, but I never brought myself to ask the question.

Cleo had calmed down. She was slowly sipping apple juice.

Before I could catch myself, I said, "I don't believe we have the same father."

"We don't look alike, but you are my brother!"

"And you are my sister!"

I reached for a breadstick. "I need to tell you something."

She stared at me.

"You remember Mr. Robby?"

Her eyes grew wide. "The undertaker's helper. The man who bought eggs and gave us stuff?"

"Yeah. He and Mom were carrying on."

"How do you know?"

"I saw them in our house, sitting in the dining room, one Saturday while Daddy was in town."

She shook her head in disbelief.

"Cleo, I sometimes wonder who Timothy's father is."

Just then, I heard the phone ring. Cleo went to answer it. That was the last thing I remembered before her gentle shake awakened me.

I was stretched out on the couch, lying under a heavy, dark blanket. In front of me, three folding tables were arranged with food. It smelled so good that I couldn't wait to eat.

"How long have I been out?"

"Almost two hours. That was Michael on the phone."

"Everything okay?"

"Yeah. He's coming over tomorrow. Are you spending the night?"

"I am."

"Why don't you join us for brunch and a movie?"

"I've got to be at work by eight o'clock."

"Can't you call Mr. Rosenberg and take the day off?"

I'd never taken a day off since I started working at the supermarket. I really wanted to meet Michael. But I needed to get home because Lola would be at Aunt Rosa's.

"You know the supermarket is busy on Saturdays."

"Okay, but I hope you change your mind." She gestured toward the food. "I ordered turkey, ham, and cheese sandwiches, a Caesar salad, cupcakes, and ice cream for dessert."

"Sounds good."

"Oh, I got a bottle of wine chilling." She grinned devilishly.

"Whoa, Only Sister! Let me wash my hands."

Cleo put on music.

"Who's that?" I asked between bites of my sandwich.

"Miles' 'So Near So Far' from his *Seven Steps to Heaven* album."

I started bobbing.

"So when's the last time you saw Rita Ann?" Cleo suddenly asked.

"I don't see her too often."

"She called a few days ago." Cleo took a sip of wine.

"How is she?"

"She filed to take exams with the Bureau of Child Welfare, the Board of Education, and the Health Department."

I smiled and took a sip of wine. I knew Rita Ann would use those papers I purchased for her.

"You don't like Rita Ann?"

"Now where did that come from?"

"We both know she likes you. She's always had a thing for you."

I chuckled.

"I'm thinking you don't care for her."

"She's nice, but Lola rocks me. She's the other reason I need to get home. She's coming to visit Aunt Rosa, and I want to see her."

Cleo put on another album. The first few bars of a saxophone perked me up.

"Who's on tenor?" I asked.

"Dexter Gordon."

"Oh?" I reached for the album cover.

"He's so cool. He lived on the West Coast for years. He was a druggie, but he kicked the habit and got himself together. He left to play in Europe and never returned. When I'm in Europe, I'm going to track him down."

I gazed at Cleo.

"In less than three months, I'll be in Europe."

"You think you'll marry Michael, Cleo?"

She looked as if she'd been struck.

"Well, is it a possibility?"

"I don't think I'll marry Michael, but it's not because he's white."

I started feeling anxious and took another sip of wine.

"I sometimes don't think I'll marry anyone."

I was too surprised to respond.

"Michael would make a good husband. He's reliable. Professionally, he's going places. He wants a big house somewhere, two dogs, a station wagon, and kids." She took a sip of wine. "It all sounds idyllic, romantic, and American perfect. But that's not what I want, and it's not what I'm about."

"What do you want? And what are you about?"

She was silent for a while.

"I want to be free."

"Free?" I repeated.

"I'm not conventional. I'm not complacent."

"What does that mean?"

"It means I want to buy clothes, listen to music late at night, and travel."

"What about work? How do you plan on making a living?"

"I'm proud I work in an office, but I hate my job. I can type sixty words a minute with no errors. I can take dictation, too. But I'll never be more than a receptionist if I stay there."

The hurt in her voice was clear, and I gently touched her arm.

"I'm going to college or some school to learn something. I don't like a nine-to-five job." She bit into a breadstick. "It's going to take time to do the things I want to do, and I'm not getting married until I'm good and ready."

I didn't respond.

"Kids made fun of the way I dressed. I stood on the free lunch line. It was embarrassing. Hell, our mother couldn't even buy me shoes that fit!"

I looked at her feet and started remembering. I understood what she was saying.

*   *   *

Bernard, Raymond, and I had been chasing each other up and down one hot afternoon in July, two months before Cleo's thirteenth birthday. That's when Duke John, Raymond's father, who drove a truck for Miles Shoe Store, came struggling up the walkway with two large cardboard boxes.

"Come help me," he said

Together, we dragged the boxes into the elevator.

Miss Connie, Duke's wife, met us at the apartment door. "What you got this time, D?"

"Ain't had time to check."

"I'm going call Bernard's mother," Miss Connie said. "I bet she wants to look."

"I need buyers. I've got to give the dispatcher and the manager their cut. Buddy, your mom and sister at home?"

"Yeah, Mr. Duke."

"Tell them I got merchandise. Knock on Rosa's door. Tell her, too."

Within minutes, the John's apartment was full of excited people.

"This box got some jazzy sandals," said Miss Florence, who with her sister, Miss Beverly, lived down the hall from the Johns.

"Let me look, too," Miss Beverly said. She started searching in the box.

"These black wedges are a size nine," Bernard's mother said.

"Yeah, but they too old looking," Aunt Rosa explained.

"You see anything, Cleo?" asked Miss Connie. She slipped her feet into a pair of gold mules.

"No. My feet are narrow. These shoes are too wide. Too loose."

Bernard's mother looked at Cleo's feet. "She got fancy feet."

"Yeah, her got Miss Ann feet," Aunt Rosa said, nodding.

"Cleo could find shoes in a swanky store," Miss Beverly advised.

"I ain't got that kind of money," Mom said.

*   *   *

Cleo refreshed our drinks. "I know you're going to be a successful writer, and I'm going to stop feeling ashamed that I once lived in the projects."

I reached for her hand. "We lived in the projects because we had to."

"Well, at least there was hot water and lots of heat."

I hugged her. She gave me her dimpled smile.

"You sound better, Cleo. You were so upset over the phone."

"Talking with you helped."

I glanced at my watch. It was past midnight.

We sat talking, listening to music, sipping wine, and eating ice cream until Cleo went to bed. I fell asleep again on the sofa.

When the dawn light woke me, I washed my face, tiptoed by the closed bedroom door, grabbed my coat and book bag, and left to catch the train back to Brooklyn.

Chapter Four
The Supermarket and Home

I went directly from Cleo's to the supermarket. I was clocking in when Mr. Rosenberg walked over with his coffee cup in hand.

Saul Rosenberg, a short, chubby, pleasant man, lived in the Canaries section of Brooklyn with his wife and nine-year-old daughter. He was a perpetual coffee drinker, and he collected withered vegetables from the produce department for his daughter's guinea pigs. The supermarket was huge, serving several housing developments and the surrounding area, and it sold more than food. There was a stamp machine, and folks could purchase the *Daily News*. To Mr. Rosenberg's credit, he hired locals, young men especially. The place was spotless.

"Oh, you got my message." He said and took a sip of coffee.

"What message?"

"I called your home late Friday and spoke with a man. Charles. I asked him to tell you to get in earlier this morning."

"Everything all right, Mr. Rosenberg?"

"Couldn't be better, Buddy. I want to talk with you about taking on check cashing."

I removed my coat and waited for him to continue.

"Chuck Graves and I talked it over. We need someone to approve checks for cashing. You're a good cashier. Your drawer is never short, and you know how to handle people, so we want you to have a shot at it. What do you think?"

Mr. Graves was the district manager. I knew he respected me, but I never expected this.

"What's involved?"

"Well, you know most customers come in with checks the first and the fifteenth of the month."

Many folks received pension, unemployment, social security, and welfare checks on the first and the fifteenth. And I was thinking about the discounts he offered those times. I had been responsible for posting flyers that announced the specials. I glanced at the flyers, which listed the current sales that were waiting for me that day.

"Yes, I know."

"I've been giving approval, but it's time consuming and takes me away from other duties. Chuck and I want you to do it. Help customers fill out a check-cashing card, photograph them, issue photo ID cards, and file everything. When you're not doing that, you'll be on the cash register."

I was wondering how much of a salary increase these new responsibilities would bring.

"You'll graduate in June, right?"

"That's correct."

"Who knows what may be ahead for you? The chain is growing. We'll need managers and supervisors. Chuck has some innovative ideas. He's negotiating with Con Edison and the telephone company. He's hoping customers will pay those bills here. He also met with the local assemblyman to talk about setting up a voter registration booth."

I knew Chuck Graves had juice, but I didn't know it was to that extent.

"What kind of salary increase and other benefits are you offering?"

"We'll increase your salary two dollars an hour."

I couldn't believe what I had just heard. I would be making over three dollars an hour, but I would work hard for every penny.

"You'll also receive a 10 percent discount on purchases. If you join us full time after you graduate, we could offer two weeks of vacation plus sick days and an additional increase."

"You know, I've never been absent or late since the day I was employed. I often work past quitting time, but I've never asked for or received overtime."

He gulped his coffee and made a face.

"I'll give it a try, but I want a $2.50 an hour increase."

Mr. Rosenberg laughed and reached for my hand. "You got it. Now can you get those flyers up?"

"You bet."

* * *

I posted the flyers. Ed, a policeman moonlighting as a security guard, opened the doors, and customers started coming in. Mr. Rosenberg signaled for me to come to his office, a raised, enclosed platform in a corner of the big supermarket. He handed me a large package of index cards.

"For the customers' information." He smiled.

I grabbed a card and created an outline that included name, address, phone number, date of birth, identification, check number, date, and the bank it was drawn on. I handed the card to Mr. Rosenberg. He looked at my creation and nodded approvingly.

He unlocked a steel file cabinet and pulled out a beat-up Polaroid.

"It's loaded, but I think you're going to have a busy day." He chuckled and tossed two packs of film my way.

Ed came hurrying over. "Mr. Rosenberg," he said with a sense of urgency. "You ready? Folks are here to cash checks."

"Send them to Buddy. That's his job now."

Ed smiled and slapped me a high five. I set up a folding table and two chairs next to the soda, candy, and cigarette vending machines and took a seat. A woman arrived with two grandchildren and a shopping cart. She pulled her social security check from her bosom and handed it to me. She had difficulty reading. She had forgotten her glasses, so I assisted her.

More customers came. The elderly women, many with canes, appeared to enjoy the attention of having their photo taken and filling out a card. I took two photos, attached the store's copy to the index card, and placed the card alphabetically in the metal card file. The other photo would be laminated and mailed to the customer.

Younger, talkative, and flirtatious women presented their employment, unemployment, and welfare checks. They refreshed their lipstick, rearranged their hair, and positioned themselves just so before they allowed me to take their pictures. Many men, accompanied by wives and girlfriends, pulled government, disability, and unemployment checks from worn leather wallets and stared at the camera.

And so it went. Ed added two more chairs, and I added an ashtray to my table. Restless children asked for money to buy snacks from the vending machine, and men gave women their seats. Folks saw I was doing what Mr. Rosenberg once did. They smiled and nodded. Several patted me on the back. I felt proud, and I worked harder.

Midway through the day, I had just left the men's room when a brassy voice behind me said, "Well, if it ain't B."

I turned and saw MaryAlice Sanchez, a girl I had known since junior high school, with several people I didn't recognize. Their shopping carts were filled with party goods, paper plates, colorful napkins, and packages of plastic forks, knives, and spoons.

"MaryAlice!" I said. "What's going on?"

She tossed her blonde-streaked, brown hair, and solemnly replied, "What does it matter to you? You don't call or return calls. So I thought you had developed amnesia."

"Girl, it ain't like that." She stared at me. "You know I'm cool."

"Well, I hope you're cool enough to come to the party I'm giving tonight. My cousin, Jay." She nodded toward the taller of the two guys. "He turned twenty-one yesterday."

"MaryAlice, I've got something planned for the weekend."

I remembered how she and I had shared some good times, but I had no ride. My pockets weren't deep, and she had disappeared last summer. Word was that she had been pregnant and sent to Puerto Rico to have an abortion. I'd never take chances with MaryAlice or anyone. And although she was sultry and available, I didn't trust her and kept my distance.

She fluttered thick lashes and gave me a knowing look. "B, you can bring her."

And her posse broke out in laughter.

"I just may do that," I replied.

"Bet," she said and sashayed away.

I glanced at my watch. It was three thirty. I wondered what movie Cleo and Michael were planning to see, and I thought I should check out what was playing at the Loew's theater on Pitkin Avenue, not too far from where I lived. Maybe after a shower and a few winks, I would take Lola to the movies. Afterward, we could check out MaryAlice's party.

There was no line. I dashed into the office and quickly dialed Aunt Rosa's number, but there was no answer. I was about to dial my number when I saw Miss Hazel, Rita Ann's mother, pushing a shopping cart piled with food.

"Hey, I was looking for your checkout line, but Ed said you've gotten a promotion. Congratulations."

"Miss Hazel, I'm just learning."

"Well, how's your brother? He all right?"

I suddenly realized I hadn't seen or spoken to him or Mom in a day or so.

"Sure, sure. He's fine."

I thought, "Why is she asking about Timothy?"

"Well, did they keep him? Or are they going to send him home?"

"Keep him? Keep him where?" I glanced up to see a customer approaching with a check in hand.

"Buddy, you don't know?" Miss Hazel eyed me over the rim of her pink-and-white rhinestone glasses.

"Know what? What am I supposed to know?"

I thought, "Dreary woman, what are you talking about?"

"Folks say cops were called to your apartment. An ambulance took Timothy to Kings County."

I'm not sure what my reaction was, but the next thing I knew, she was holding my hand.

"Buddy, you all right?"

"I think so. What happened to Timothy?"

"I don't know. Rita Ann went over your place to check out things. As soon as I finish shopping, I'm going, too. What time you getting off?"

I glanced at my watch. The customer was waiting.

"When I'm finished with this customer."

"Well, I'll see you there."

Timothy's asthma had appeared under control. He was eating better. He was going to school.

"What happened to him?" I thought.

Miss Hazel hadn't mentioned Charles or Mom.

"Where were they?" I thought.

With a huge rush of guilt, I realized that, after dropping Timothy at Aunt Rosa's, I'd never called to check on him. Cleo and I had gotten so wrapped up that I hadn't thought of my brother, and she hadn't asked about him.

By four fifteen, fifteen minutes past my quitting time, I had finished with the last customer. I usually stayed a few minutes longer, but not today. Giving Mr. Rosenberg a nod, I handed him all the material and clocked out. I hailed a gypsy cab.

I showed the driver a twenty and said, "Make every light."

* * *

There was still daylight remaining when the cab pulled up in front of my building. A crowd of Timothy's friends rushed over when they saw me. They were all speaking at once.

"How is he?"

"He all right?"

"What happened to him?"

"I'm checking it out." I moved quickly inside the building. I was relieved to see no one in the lobby and an empty elevator waiting because I didn't know how I would respond to more inquiries.

Someone had dropped a carton of eggs in the elevator. The shells crackling under my feet grated my already overwrought nerves. The sticky yolks fastened to my loafers. I recalled how spotless Cleo's place was.

"One day, I'll live someplace else," I thought.

I was surprised to see Aunt Rosa entering my apartment. She was carrying our garbage can. I heard running water and smelled ammonia.

"What's going on?" I asked her.

"The apartment was a mess, and we cleaned it up."

"What happened? And where is my mother?"

"Clara Mae is sleeping. The doctor gave her some medicine."

I stepped into our apartment and saw Miss Hazel mopping our living room floor.

"Buddy, you got here fast!"

Lola and Rita Ann emerged from the kitchen. Lola's head was covered with a scarf, and she wore faded jeans. The sleeves of her white blouse were rolled up. On her hands were yellow plastic gloves.

"Buddy, I'm glad to see you," she said.

I gave her a quick nod. "What's going on here?"

"Auntie and I cleaned up. Rita Ann cooked," Lola replied.

"What? I don't understand. When I left this place Friday, everything was fine. Now you all," I said, gesturing toward Lola and Aunt Rosa, "are telling me you had to clean up. Clean up after what?"

Rita Ann was busy placing bowls of potato salad, lima beans, and a platter of fried chicken on the table. I waited for someone to answer my question.

"I had just come home from the beauty parlor 'cause I'm going to MaryAlice's party. Mama told me that Miss Rosa called and said the cops had taken Timothy to the hospital and your mother to the police station," Rita Ann said.

I was too shaken to speak.

Rita Ann continued, "Mama asked me to go over to your house and check things out while she went food shopping. Beer bottles, cigarettes, and cigar butts were everywhere."

"Where was Charles?" I asked.

"There was no sign of him." Rita Ann replied.

"Tell me what happened, Aunt Rosa."

She stopped eating long enough to say, "Timothy stayed with me a good while after you dropped him off Friday. He ate, and he was watching TV."

"Wait a minute. Mom was getting off at four o'clock. She didn't come and get him?"

Aunt Rosa wiped her mouth. "Charles did. He come knocking on my door hard."

"Mr. Rosenberg said he called last night and gave Charles a message to give me."

Aunt Rosa wiped her mouth again. "Yes, he was waiting for your mama. I think he had plans to do something with her. But when she didn't show up, he came looking for her at my place."

"What happened then?"

"He got really mad, took Timothy, and left."

"What happened to Timothy?"

"I don't know 'cause I went to sleep. About seven o'clock this morning, Lola called to tell me what time she was coming."

Lola nodded.

Aunt Rosa slurped her tea. "I heard voices. Clara Mae was yelling and screaming. I opened my door and saw her in the hall in her nightgown. She was pulling on Charles and begging him not to leave. She was crying and saying how much she loved him." Aunt Rosa sat her cup down. "I see him pushing your mother off. He says to her, 'Go deal with your sorry son.' And he headed to the elevator."

"Well, what happened next?" I asked.

"I don't know. I tried to get Clare Mae to calm down 'cause she was crying something terrible. I tried to get her back in the apartment. She was in the hallway half-dressed, you understand. The neighbors were looking."

Lola rubbed my hand. Aunt Rosa took a bite of chicken.

"When I get in this place, I can't believe what I see. Beer cans were all over, and they had been partying 'cause the smell of reefer was strong. I see Timothy. He on the phone. He the one that called them cops. I don't know what he say, but they got here mighty fast."

"I'm going to wake up Mom."

But Aunt Rosa grabbed my arm. "Let me finish telling you what happened."

I sat back down.

"This place filled up with cops. They talking to Clara Mae. I see them shaking their heads. The main one, the big white one with them stripes on his sleeves, told her to get ready. He called an ambulance. They put Timothy on the stretcher and left here some kind of fast."

I was speechless.

"We need to find out what happened," Lola said.

I dashed to the bathroom and washed my face. I needed a

shower and a shave badly, but seeing Timothy was more important. I gently knocked on Mom's door. When there was no
response, I opened it. The covers were pulled tightly over her
head, and I could hear her heavy breathing. I decided not to
wake her after all. I softly closed the door and headed to the
kitchen.

"I'm headed to Kings County," I said.

"Take this chicken sandwich," Rita Ann insisted as I rushed
for the door.

"Rita Ann, you are a real friend."

"Buddy, you are special. Anything I can do while you are
gone?"

"Pray," I replied. Then I opened the door.

* * *

At Kings County, I was directed to pediatric emergency. At
the register, I gave Timothy's name and date of birth.

"Who are you?" asked the fast-talking clerk.

"I'm Benson Lee Powell Jr. His brother."

"You have any identification?"

I presented my high school lunch card. The clerk glanced at
the photo.

"How old are you?"

"Nineteen."

"Where are your parents? Are your mother and father here?"

"My father is deceased. My mother is at home."

"I have to call my supervisor." She picked up the phone.

I gawked at her.

"Please take a seat," she said and dialed a number.

The overwhelming odor of disinfectant made me nauseous,
so I dug in my bag and began eating the sandwich Rita Ann had
given me, hoping to keep myself from getting sick. The place

was busy. Doctors and nurses darted in and out of dull, green-and-yellow examination rooms. Women holding babies sat on hard benches. They smoked, talked, and waited to be called. The address system continuously paged doctors. I went to a vending machine to buy a soda. Telephones were nearby, and I lost three dimes before finding one that worked. I dialed Cleo's number, but I got a busy signal. I dialed my home, but there was no answer, so I dialed Aunt Rosa's. She picked up on the first ring.

"We left your place about an hour ago. Your mama was still sleeping."

"Thanks. Let me speak to Lola."

When Lola came on the line, she sounded anxious. "Buddy, is your brother all right? Did you see him?"

"I haven't seen him yet. I still don't know if he's okay. I'm waiting to speak with someone."

"Keep us informed."

I glanced at my watch. It was seven thirty.

"I was invited to that party Rita Ann was talking about," I said to Lola. "I was going to ask if you wanted to go. But now I wouldn't think of it."

"There will be other times for us, but Rita Ann is going to go."

I was about to hang up, but I asked, "Isn't it strange that Mom is still sleeping?"

"Yes, but I checked on her. And I read the label on the medication. It's Valium."

"Why was she given that?"

"It helps people relax. Auntie said your mama and Charles had been drinking and smoking marijuana, which could intensify the medication."

"Is Mom going to be all right?"

"I checked her pulse and listened to her breathing. Everything seemed fine, but I'll check her again."

"Thanks, Lola."

"I've got to go," I said, hearing my name being paged. "But I need your help. I called Cleo right before I called you, and her line was busy. Can you call and tell her that we need to talk?"

I gave Lola the number and rushed to the registration area. A pudgy, dark-complexioned man wearing a red tie and brown jacket was standing next to the clerk. His nametag read "Leroy Jefferson."

"Are you Benson Lee Powell Jr.?" he asked in a pensive tone.

"I am."

"Where are your parents?"

I used every ounce of self-control I could find to keep from raising my voice. "Mr. Jefferson," I said, looking straight into his eyes, "I already told the receptionist that my father is dead, and my mother is at home. I want to see my brother."

"You're nineteen years old. You're not of legal age. You're not twenty-one."

"I need to see my brother!"

"Shall I call security?" the clerk asked.

Mr. Jefferson shook his head no. A flash of recognition crossed his face.

"You work in that big supermarket in Brownsville," he said. "You authorized my check for cashing today. Your name is Buddy."

"Yes, sir."

Mr. Jefferson quietly took my arm and pulled me aside, lowering his voice to a whisper.

"Social Services and the cops talked to your brother. He will be kept for observation."

Stunned, I thought, "What had happened that no one wanted to talk about?"

"I'm going to allow you to see your brother," Mr. Jefferson said, still whispering. "You have any other family members?"

"Cleo, my sister, is twenty-two," I stammered.

"If you are questioned, say she is on her way. Timothy is in room J6. It's right down the hall."

He patted my back and left. I raced down the hall. A policeman was standing at the room's entrance.

I immediately said, "I'm Benson Lee Powell, Jr., Timothy Henry Powell's brother."

He nodded.

From behind the curtains, I heard Timothy shout, "Buddy! Buddy!"

I pulled the curtains apart. My brother was sitting in a large, steel frame bed. The bars had been pulled up, and he looked as if he were in a cage. He quickly released the red toy truck he held, threw his arms up, and grabbed me. His tears came fast, and he kept calling my name. The policeman must have notified the doctors and the police because several policemen and doctors appeared.

"What happened to you?" I hugged him as I tried to hold back my own tears.

He cried and coughed. A nurse rushed over with a pill in a small, white paper cup.

"What happened to you? Why are you here?'

"Buddy," he said, sobbing, "Charles tried to put his pee-pee in my do-do."

* * *

A hand touched my shoulder.

"Mr. Benson, I'm Dr. Marion, the resident on duty."

I shook his hand, but my mind was frozen, unable to process what Timothy had just told me.

"Is it true?" I asked. "Was my brother sexually assaulted?'

Dr. Marion thumbed through the chart in his hand. "According to Dr. Katz, the intern who examined him, your brother presented with symptoms consistent with molestation. We will keep him for observation. I'm waiting for a bed."

For a few seconds, I couldn't speak. I finally said, "I want to spend time with him."

"He was given a sedative. The social worker and police are waiting to talk with you."

A somber-faced white policeman got to the point. "I'm Sergeant McGreevy. Your brother has made serious allegations against a Charles Wilkins. Captain Mallow questioned your mother in the presence of Miss Winfield, the social worker. Then Mrs. Powell was taken to the 73rd precinct to fill out papers. Is she here?"

"No. She's at home."

McGreevy eyed me sternly. "How old are you?"

"I'm nineteen."

"Is there a father or another family member I can speak with?"

I was about to answer when I heard a quick knock. A woman who reminded me of the librarian at the library entered. Her silver hair was limp and dull-looking.

Sergeant McGreevy nodded. "This is Miss Winfield. She will speak with you."

Her broad smile calmed me down. "You are Benson Lee Powell Jr.? Timothy Henry Powell's brother?"

"Yes."

"Benson," she began.

"You can call me Buddy," I interrupted.

She nodded. "Buddy, your brother's allegations are serious."

I was silent, waiting.

"Your mother stated that the accusations are false."

"My brother is not a liar, Miss Winfield. Dr. Marion said physical evidence supported his claim."

Miss Winfield looked at me intently. "Your mother appeared confused. Do you know what happened?"

"I was at work when I first learned something had happened to my brother. I rushed home. I didn't speak to my mother, but I know my brother is telling the truth."

Miss Winfield glanced through her papers. "Do you know Charles Wilkins?"

"I met him in March at my mother's birthday party. In early April, my sister, Cleo, moved out, and he moved in."

"Do you know where he lived before? Do you know where he works?"

I suddenly realized how little I knew about Charles.

"Mom told me she met him here in this hospital's housekeeping department, where she works."

Miss Winfield spoke slowly, "Yes, that's what she told us, but human resources has no record of a Charles Wilkins being employed here."

I was too dazed to respond.

"Timothy will be kept for observation. Then he will be placed in foster care."

"Foster care?"

"We have to determine if his home is safe before he can return. The police and Social Services will speak to your mother again."

Miss Winfield spent the next few minutes checking information, including Mom's name, address, and phone number. She requested the name and address of a nonresidential relative. I gave the Manhattan address and phone number where Cleo was staying. Miss Winfield then gave me her card and gathered her papers to leave.

"What's going to happen now?" I asked.

"Sergeant McGreevy will speak with you again."

I eyed the phone. "Can I call my sister?"

"Yes, of course," she said. She quietly closed the door behind her.

Cleo picked up immediately.

"Hi, Buddy!"

"Your line has been busy a long time."

"I've been talking to Michael. You got out of here real early this morning, but I slept until Michael called. Did you get to work on time?" Before I could reply, she continued. "After a champagne brunch, Michael wanted to see *The Spy Who Came in from the Cold*. He read the book, and he loves Richard Burton. But I wanted to see *Inside Daisy Clover* with Natalie Wood. I think she is so pretty and talented."

"Cleo, stop! Let me tell you what's been happening."

"What?"

"I'm at the hospital."

"You're at the hospital?"

"Yes, Kings County."

"Why?"

"Because of Timothy."

"What happened?"

"He will be admitted."

"Did he have an asthma attack? Is he all right?"

"No, he didn't have an asthma attack. I hope he will be all right."

"What do you mean? What's wrong with Timothy?"

"He said Charles tried to put his pee-pee in his do-do."

"What?"

"Timothy doesn't lie!"

"When did it happen?"

"Late last night or early this morning. I'm still putting the pieces together. Miss Hazel came shopping late this afternoon. She told me Timothy had been taken to the hospital. I saw him a while ago. He told me what Charles did. Dr. Marion, the resident, confirmed it."

"And where was Mom while this was going on?"

"She was at home. Aunt Rosa said she and Charles had been drinking and smoking marijuana."

"What?"

"Timothy called the police."

"Timothy called the police?"

"He did."

"Where is that Charles bastard now?"

"He left. Aunt Rosa said he and Mom were arguing in the hallway. Mom was in her nightgown. Aunt Rosa heard her telling Charles that she loved him and begging him to stay."

"Let me speak to her."

"She's at home, sleeping."

"Sleeping," Cleo repeated in disbelief.

"She was given medication."

"What a mess!" Cleo whispered.

"It gets worse."

"How so?"

"The social worker said Mom said Timothy was lying."

Cleo gasped.

"I need to speak to the police again."

I was about to share with her everything I knew, but Cleo screamed, "I'm jumping in a cab. I'm coming to you and Mom."

I left the hospital and hurried home.

Chapter Five
The Facts

I was surprised to see Mom sitting on the sofa when I entered the apartment, but her appearance distressed me. Her hair was matted. Her grayish white gown scarcely covered her thighs, and her feet hung out of her frayed, colorless slippers. I was stunned to hear her slurred voice.

"I need a cigarette," she said.

"What!"

Her bloodshot eyes scrutinized me, and I stared back.

"Timothy is in the hospital, but you're asking about cigarettes! Do you know why he called the police?"

"That medicine made me shaky. I need to clear my head." She started searching through the ashtray for a butt.

"Well, cigarettes won't help you!"

She gave me a drop-dead look and scratched her head. "Well, is he all right?"

"You tell me what happened to my brother?"

She rubbed her nose with the back of her hand. "Timothy and Charles got into it."

"What do you mean? What did they get into?"

"I can't think straight. I can't remember."

"Try."

She started coughing. "Charles was mad."

"Why?"

"Timmy wanted to watch the Charlie Brown and Snoopy special, but Charles wanted to watch something else. Charles ordered Timothy to bed."

"And Charles molested him!"

"No, Charles watched TV!"

"What about the drinking, the beer, and the grass?'

"Yeah, we started partying."

My anger was rising as I listened to her dull voice.

"We ate and drank beer. Charles had weed."

I moved closer. "Timothy was here. You and Charles acted like fools!"

"Smart mouth! This is my house!"

"And Timothy is my brother, and that creep Charles sexually assaulted him."

"Charles didn't touch him!"

"You were so out of it that you couldn't have known what he did!"

"Hush your mouth," she whispered. Her face was dark with anger.

"No! I won't be quiet! You didn't protect Timothy! And you couldn't protect Cleo from being bothered by those horrible men when we lived in that hotel."

Without warning, Mom grabbed the glass ashtray from the coffee table and lunged forward.

"Watch your mouth!" she yelled.

As she swung and hit my jaw, the door opened.

"Mom, have you lost your mind?" Cleo shouted, dropping her bag and running to snatch the ashtray from our mother's hand.

Mom's eyes were blazing. "Buddy sassed me!"

Aunt Rosa and Lola rushed in.

Mom shouted, "Buddy's mouth is too fresh!"

"My mouth spoke the truth. Something you don't want to hear!"

"Lord, what is going on?" Aunt Rosa asked, gasping.

Lola hurried over to examine my face. "Nothing is broken.

The skin isn't bruised." She took my pulse and whispered, "We heard screaming and rushed over."

I leaned my head on her chest.

"Mom, you've gone too far," Cleo said. She turned to Aunt Rosa. "Get her in the bedroom."

"Buddy, what happened?" Cleo's eyes were calm, but her voice was tense.

"I came home after seeing Timothy, and she was on the sofa. She asked about cigarettes, not Timothy!"

Cleo sighed.

"I asked her what happened to him. She claimed she couldn't remember, but she did say Charles hadn't touched Timothy."

Lola led me toward the kitchen table and placed a glass of water in front of me. "I bet the liquor, beer, and marijuana distorted your mother's memory."

Aunt Rosa hurried over. "She's back in bed, but she keeps asking for cigarettes. Cleo, give her one of yours."

Cleo was busy making coffee. She quickly said, "I don't smoke anymore."

I gave Cleo a knowing glance, but Aunt Rosa and Lola stared at her. I didn't know if it was weariness, hunger, tension, or the humiliation I felt after being struck by Mom (or a combination of them all), but I suddenly had an intense headache.

"I need to get back to the hospital," I said.

"I'm going with you," Cleo said. She grabbed her purse.

I picked up my book bag and headed for the door. I thought of the ugly incident. If Cleo hadn't arrived, I wondered what I could have done. I'd never hit anyone, not even the school bullies who teased me. Words were my weapons. I had a way with them, even when I couldn't read. My tongue had gained me respect and kept me free of physical confrontations. What had just happened was ugly. But I knew Mom was unable to listen. Her hitting me was an attempt to silence what she didn't want to hear.

Cleo and I headed out the door. The loud sounds of pots and pans followed us.

"We'll have food waiting when you all return," Lola said.

We started walking toward the elevator and heard clicking sounds. I recognized it as heels. Our mother was rushing in our direction. She had pulled her hair into a bun, and she wore a bright red rhinestone jacket. Her silver bag swung as she was running. I braced myself, not knowing what to expect.

"I'm coming, too! I think I need to find out what really happened to my child."

* * *

At the hospital, we were told that Timothy had been moved. We took the elevator. Riding up, Mom stood silently between Cleo and me and held our hands. I didn't know how to react, so I remained quiet.

"I'm Cleola Mae Powell," Cleo said to the clerk at the nurse's station. "I'm here with my mother and my brother. We want to speak with Dr. Marion and see Timothy Henry Powell."

"Take a seat in the waiting room. I'll page him."

The waiting area was painted a drab gray. Soda, candy, and cigarette machines were lined up against one wall. When Cleo started digging in her large leather purse, I knew what she was about to do. She dropped thirty-five cents in the cigarette machine's coin slot, pushed the button labeled Parliament, and gave the pack to Mom.

"Thank you," Mom said in a voice slightly above a whisper. She looked like a grateful child.

She walked over to the window, slowly opened the pack of cigarettes, took one out, and lit it. There was a distant look in her eyes as she exhaled. I watched for a while before I slowly walked over to her. I didn't know what I was going to say or what to expect from her, but I wanted to talk. She knew I was standing there, but she refused to acknowledge me. And I was losing my nerve. Suddenly, she turned and looked at me, but she appeared dazed. I softly touched her arm. She blinked rapidly and coughed.

In a low voice, I asked, "Mom, can you tell me what happened to Timothy?"

She lowered her eyes. She seemed too ashamed to look at me. I waited.

Her voice was almost inaudible. "Buddy, I'm sorry I hit you."

"Mom," I began.

But she interrupted. "I didn't want to hear what you said. I didn't watch out for Cleo. I've said mean things to you."

"Mom."

But she interrupted again. "I ain't been around when Timothy needed me."

"What happened to him?'

"I don't know. I was high!" She started to cry. Cleo rushed over with tissues. "I've been so bad and—"

"Mom," Cleo stated to speak, but Mom interrupted her.

"Cleo, you is pretty and smart. You is a high school graduate. I is ugly and a toilet bowl cleaner."

Cleo seemed astonished to hear those words. Mom's eyes fell on me.

"You will graduate in June."

"Mom!" Cleo and I said at once.

"I got through sixth grade, and that was big back then. Colored kids dropped out in the third or fourth grade. Had to pick cotton and care for their mamas and their mama's babies. But Old Man Valentine took a liking to me. He owned the land we sharecropped, and he told the man I called Daddy to keep me in school."

"Old Man Valentine? Sheriff Valentine's father? He helped you?" I asked in amazement.

"He had power. Things were soon all right 'cause he had me."

Cleo turned red. I was too surprised to respond.

"I can guess what you thinking," Mom said dryly. "I bet you done heard the stories about white men taking advantage of colored girls in the South. But Old Man Valentine didn't do nothing to me I didn't want done."

Cleo looked faint. I rubbed her back.

"I knew folks who knew things. For a few dollars, Cleo, you could have been jerked from my body, put in the slop jar, and dumped in the river to feed the fish. But you were wanted."

I was thinking how often I had wondered who Cleo's father was and if it disturbed her that she and I were half-brother and half-sister. Now we knew who her dad was, and I speculated whom Timothy's father might be. I recalled what I saw happen between Mom and Mr. Robby.

"Old Man Valentine died. I was left, high and dry, poor and hungry, with Cleo to feed and clothe. I was young and fine, so I married you and Timothy's papa, Buddy."

I listened to her with suspicion and doubt. Cleo wiped her face with the tissues she had brought for Mom.

Mom's voice became soft. "I wasn't faithful. Senior was good. I wasn't."

I took hers and Cleo's hands. I could see unquestionable sorrow in Mom's eyes as she looked from me to Cleo.

"I don't know what happened when Charles told Timothy to go to bed. But I think Charles went in that bedroom, too."

I cringed. Cleo sobbed.

"I woke up on the sofa, and Timothy was crying."

Mom released my hand. "Buddy, I didn't protect Timothy. When you said what you said, I went off." She looked at me. Her look was so forlorn that I wanted to cry.

Cleo gently wiped Mom's nose. "I'm glad you're here with us."

I slowly shook my head. "Cleo, it's been hell."

I filled them in on the discussions I'd had with Dr. Marion, Sergeant McGreevy, and Miss Winfield. Mom gasped when she heard Timothy would be placed in foster care.

"I need to get myself together," she whispered.

To her credit, Mom had often tried to stop drinking. She frequently remained sober for two to three weeks. But, with the least bit of frustration, like an unexpected change in her work schedule, a letter from school about Timothy, or a fight with one of her male friends, it would prompt her to pour a drink.

"Maybe this is the wake-up call you needed. Now you can get help. Maybe you'll attend AA," I slowly said.

"I've been trying to stop. I want to stop. There's stuff I don't want to do. All the partying, the lying, and hanging out ain't right. You know, Charles didn't work at Kings County. He never did. I don't even know if he had a job."

Cleo's sobbing was growing louder. Mom looked like a trapped animal.

"I bet Charles Wilkins isn't even his real name," I said.

Just as I was about to ask Mom where she had met Charles, Dr. Marion walked in.

"Mr. Benson," he said, shaking my hand.

"Dr. Marion, this is my sister Cleola and our mother, Mrs. Powell."

"How is Timothy?" Cleo asked between sobs. "Is he going to be all right?"

"He just woke up and—"

Before Dr. Marion could finish, Mom said, "I want to see my son."

"He is being examined by Dr. Butler, a pediatrician who specializes in this area."

Mom lowered her eyes.

"You can see him afterward."

72

"How long will he remain here?" I asked. "Is he going to be all right?"

"Dr. Butler will speak to you after he completes his examination. I'll call you."

We sat in silence. Mom smoked one cigarette after another. Cleo stared at the walls. I imagined Charles molesting Timothy, and I began sobbing, too. Cleo hugged me. Mom put her hand on my arm. Cleo leaned close to me.

"We are going to take care of our mother and our brother," she whispered next to my ear.

I exhaled slowly. I had misgivings, but I remained silent.

Chapter Six
Together

Timothy was hospitalized for two days and then placed in the home of a Staten Island foster care couple, Mr. and Mrs. Harrington. Our mother started attending counseling, parenting classes, and AA meetings at the foster care agency's request. We all visited Timothy weekly at the foster care agency's office.

Initially, he cried and begged to come home. "Buddy, I miss you. I miss my friends."

I held him as Cleo and Mom wiped his face and Mrs. Harrington squeezed his hand reassuringly. I liked Mrs. Harrington. She would saunter in, wearing a multicolored outfit and head wrap and carrying an oversized bag packed with food. The bag would be balanced expertly on one of her broad shoulders. When I visited Timothy, he would search in my pockets for treats, like baseball cards and racing cars. I would also hide Tootsie Rolls, his favorite candy, in my pockets

"Read to me! Read to me!" He would insist. "I want to hear how Furious Red won a prize after getting 100 percent on his spelling test two weeks in a row."

After reading, I would tell him how we were searching for a new place to live. I was tired of riding in funky elevators, and Cool had started getting under my skin.

"My man," he'd said recently as he slapped me five, "let me cop a couple of Lincolns."

"Hey!" I told him. "You ain't paid back the last loan I gave you."

He took a drag on his cigarette and gawked at me.

"Cool, maybe you should talk to the man at the supermarket about a J-O-B?"

A slow smirk danced around the corners of his thick lips. "Dude, I ain't got the words you got."

I told Cleo how anxious I was to move.

"We need to get out of the projects. We need a different place to bring Timothy to."

"I've put the word out," she reassured me.

Timothy, who was busily rolling the green racing car I had brought him, squealed, "Buddy, I'm on a break, right?"

"That's an interesting way of putting it." I tugged his ear.

He smiled, but his eyes were sad. "I don't ever want to go away again."

* * *

At school, we practiced for the graduation ceremony. Many of my classmates ordered the yearbook and school ring. I wasn't buying either one. The money I had saved would help with an apartment. Getting Timothy back home was what mattered to me. At the supermarket, I had learned my new responsibilities well. Mr. Rosenberg was pleased.

"Buddy, what are your plans after June?" asked Chuck Graves one day when he dropped by the store.

"Everything is up in the air, Mr. Graves."

"Call me Chuck." He smiled. "Things are changing for people like you."

I looked at him in surprise.

"There's opportunities for good, honest workers."

I smiled, but I was thinking how I needed to find more time to write. I continuously submitted my work, and a Furious Red story had recently been accepted for publication. My confidence soared when I received a check for three hundred dollars. I couldn't wait to share the news with Mom and Cleo.

Cleo had started visiting and having meals with us frequently. She kept me informed about the apartment search, and she gave Mom pep talks. But she didn't need them. Mom was changing. She keep her counseling appointments and attended AA meetings consistently. She had cut down on her smoking. She regularly made breakfast for me before I headed to school. I was proud of her and told her.

"Buddy," she said one evening when she was leaving for an AA meeting, "I'm on the right track, and I ain't getting off this time."

I gave her a reassuring hug. I said a silent prayer that she would succeed this time. I wanted my family back. I regularly fantasized about how it would be living together in a different place in Manhattan. No people would be hanging outside our building. Timothy would attend a better school. Cleo would no longer feel ashamed about where she lived and invite her new friends over. Mom would smile often. And we would all talk to each other and not yell. And there would be no liquor or cigarettes around.

A few days after my talk with Chuck Graves, I told Mom and Cleo about the check.

"Congratulations," Mom said, smiling widely.

Cleo started clapping.

"Three hundred dollars to drop in the pot for our apartment."

"By golly, chap!" Cleo said in a faux British accent. She put down her fork. "Haven't you said you wanted a leather jacket like mine?"

"Yes," I answered sheepishly. "What you getting at?"

"It's elementary, my dear Watson," she continued. "You're going to use that money to buy a jacket. I'm going to take you shopping!"

"I'm coming with you," Mom added.

We laughed so hard that my sides ached.

That Saturday, we went to Martin's, the most exclusive store in downtown Brooklyn. We strolled across carpeted floors. Salesmen addressed me like I was a big shot. They brought out jackets, and I slipped into them as easily as putting on a cashmere sweater. Cleo helped me select a midnight blue jacket. I also got a pair of slacks and a turtleneck.

We then went to Junior's in downtown Brooklyn, which was famous for its cheesecake. We were having a leisurely dinner when Mom touched my arm.

"Buddy," she said, "I want to read one of your stories."

"You've got to be kidding!" I thought.

"I'm surprised to hear you say that. You told me I couldn't even spell."

"I said that, and I apologize."

Now I was speechless.

Cleo purchased strawberries and bananas at a corner vegetable stand. Once home, Mom made coffee. We sat side by side eating and listening to Jackie Wilson, Jerry Butler, and the Impressions. Being together felt good. And the fact that no liquor or cigarettes were around made our gathering even more special.

I started thinking about how we had come north with three battered suitcases filled with tattered clothing after Daddy's death. I also remembered what Cleo had experienced when we lived in that awful hotel, my struggle to learn how to read, and now our latest trial with Timothy's placement in foster care. A recent chat with Aunt Rosa crept across my mind.

* * *

"I miss Timmy something awful," she said. "How is he doing, Buddy?"

"You wouldn't recognize him, Auntie. Mrs. Harrington takes excellent care of him. He eats her good cooking. He's gotten taller, and he's put on weight."

"Hmm, ain't that woman West Indian?"

"She's from Trinidad, but she's lived here for many years."

"And didn't I hear your mama say they got a great big house over in Staten Island, some place nobody in their right mind would live? And they brought a new Dodge station wagon?"

"They have a four-bedroom house. They got the station wagon 'cause one of their foster children uses a wheelchair. But what's the point, Auntie?"

"One of their foster children? How many they got?"

"They have two others, a teenage girl and a boy named Freddie. He's six and shares a bedroom with Timothy."

"You know, I've heard stories about those kinds of folks, people from the West Indies. They take in children for money so they can buy homes and things. I've even heard cases where they filled up the house with foster kids and don't adopt any of them 'cause they get more money that way. And your mama said the husband had a good job, too. They making plenty of money, you can believe that. Them kids are cash cows! That's all! You all better get Timothy as soon as possible!"

"Auntie, I hear your concerns, but they know Timothy is coming back home. They are good people."

"You just keep your eyes and ears open, Buddy," she said. "Oh, is Timmy going to testify at Charles' trial?"

* * *

Three weeks earlier, the phone rang as we were having dinner. Charles had been caught. Mom had given information to the police, and they had tracked him down and captured the bastard. Charles Wilkinson, whom Mom had met at a hangout, was the actual name of the forty-six-year-old drifter from Tennessee who had an arrest record that included drunk driving and allegations of child molestation.

"I really didn't know Charles before inviting him to my birthday party," she had confessed.

"He was cruising for someone like you, Mom," Cleo said.

"You got that right," I said.

"Charles had lucked out when he hooked up with a needy woman who had a job, an apartment, and a vulnerable young son," I thought.

* * *

"I don't know, Auntie. We have to wait and see. The trial is in December. By that time, we should be living in Manhattan."

"Way over there! Why you all moving to the city?"

"A friend of Cleo's located a large apartment in a nice neighborhood."

"Is Cleo still going on that trip with the white guy?"

"Yes, he purchased the tickets."

* * *

Cleo's touch brought me back to the present.

"So how about reading something?"

Before I could protest, she put down her bowl of fruit. She turned off the music, kicked off her shoes, crossed her legs, and sat closer to Mom. She looked like a child at Christmastime, and Mom's eyes were bright with anticipation. I was nervous. Timothy was the only person I had read my stories to, but I couldn't think of any excuse not to read. So I slowly thumbed through my Furious Red stories. More than a hundred were in the second book, which I was holding. The first was tucked away in the scruffy suitcase where I kept memorabilia.

I chose "Inside Toilet," a story of how Furious Red's family got an inside toilet after using an outhouse for years.

"I thought it was strange," Mom said after I finished reading the story, "the way you described how the outhouse had girly pictures on its walls."

"Yeah, who put them there?" Cleo asked. "It's inconsistent. Furious Red's father wouldn't plaster photos of naked women on the toilet's walls."

"I've got to rewrite that," I said, thinking how astute she was.

"When you described how the toilet smelled of Lysol, I thought that was right on the money though," Cleo said.

"Well, you know the stench was awful."

"Yeah," she replied. "And I bet it was no fun rushing to an outhouse when you had diarrhea."

"You are sick, Cleo," I said and laughed.

Mom almost spilled her coffee laughing. "Read another story, Buddy," she said.

I could see she was excited. In spite of myself, it made me feel proud.

I read, "Miss Michaels," a story about a healer who claimed to have the power to help folks with their financial problems. Furious Red's Mother had consulted Miss Michaels for advice concerning money.

Cleo started singing, "There's a future Pulitzer Prize winner in our family."

I was no longer uneasy.

Mom touched my arm. "You made up those stories?"

"Yeah, they're all fiction."

"Well, have you written any nonfiction?" Cleo asked.

"I have."

"Share one with us." Cleo said with anticipation.

I searched in my book bag, pulled out my journal of nonfiction stories, and slowly started turning pages. They were filled with my thoughts. Many were unpleasant. I wrote how embarrassed I'd felt that we didn't live in a nice place like many of my classmates. There were serious words about Cleo and her music. I liked most of the music she played, but I didn't know about Bob Dylan. I thought his voice was awful, although the words of his songs were poignant and right on time about the civil rights movement and all. But listening to him was painful.

I wrote about Rita Ann, but I didn't want to share those passages. I knew my sister hoped something would click between her best friend and me, but Rita Ann's complacency, dowdy appearance, and lack of interest in reading turned me off. However, when I learned she and MaryAlice's cousin, Jay, were dating and she had filed to take several Civil Service exams, I wrote how happy I was for her.

Pages were devoted to my desire to achieve money and fame. I described how a fancy car would be parked in my garage and how, with an impressive ride, money, and the right address, I could pull a fox like MaryAlice.

Right after that entry, however, I thought how Lola's long, thick hair; dark skin; and diminutive stature had turned me on. I had written how I could imagine us becoming serious further down the road.

I described how being a senior and the first male in my family to attend high school made me feel proud. I wrote about how jealous I had felt after meeting Earl Ernest Johnson. He embodied many of my desires. His parents were college alumni, he attended college, and he seemed to have it all together. Now, as I looked at those words, I felt uncomfortable about never contacting him or going to the meeting on his flyer. But I kept the flyer. I carried it with me always, and I promised myself that I'd call him.

I had even written about my art classes and how I enjoyed studying the Italian Renaissance and the works of Botticelli,

Bellini, Caravaggio, and Raphael. In every house and church I visited, there was a reproduction of *The Last Supper*. I had seen copies of the *Mona Lisa*, but I had no idea who the painters were or that they were one and the same, Leonardo da Vinci, until I studied the Italian Renaissance.

I felt an affinity toward da Vinci when I learned he had kept countless diaries and journals. In 1963, the French government had lent the *Mona Lisa* to the Metropolitan Museum in New York City, and I went on a class trip to view the masterpiece. The slight smile on the smooth face of the mysterious-looking woman had fascinated me. Afterward, I was motivated to try describing my own face, using words instead of paint. I selected that entry to read while Mom and Cleo watched me intently.

"I am going to read something I call 'My Self Face.'"

Mom smiled; Cleo placed her hands in her lap.

"My physical self face makes me want to laugh. It looks as if the chief of the face factory was away and an overzealous trainee took advantage of the situation. She flexed her muscles to create her first unsupervised face. The neophyte selected a nose from a box that was scheduled to be discarded. She reached her nervous arm over her head and grabbed a pair of eyes from a long, narrow shelf. She found a pair of lips in a tray where ears should have been, and the ears she grasped from the ear jar were the first pair her shaking hand touched. A chin was picked out of the chin container without any thought or effort. It took the apprentice less than a second to select cheeks. The novice hastily put these haphazardly selected parts in a brown burlap bag and shook the bag vigorously. Pronto! What was created was the physical self face I now wear. My eyes are too small. My mouth, lips, and nose are too wide and thick. That's my physical self face, and I've learned to accept it.

"My emotional self face is a challenge. It never displays what it really feels. It laughs when it should cry. It cries when it should scream. It is often not taken seriously when it is solemn. It is misinterpreted and labeled by some. And I am learning to be gentle with it.

"I have other self face selves. I have a financially conservative self face; I have an eager, intellectual self face. When I visit the city, I have a stoic self face. And I have a powerful angry self face I seldom display. But my best self face is one that attempts to be objective, but it acknowledges and knows it is human. Being impartial is easier said than done. My objective self face dislikes backstabbers and underhanded dealers. It is intolerant of ignorance. It is not content with complacency, and it tries to overcome mediocrity. My best self face meditates and ponders its actions and decisions. It constantly reaffirms its values and goals. It is a self face that does not lie."

I had been focused on reading. When I stopped, the silence enveloped me. It was very quiet. Mom and Cleo were wrapped in each other's arms. They didn't speak. I couldn't think of anything to say, so I sat there. But Mom reached over and stroked my face, and Cleo kissed it.

* * *

Three weeks later, Timothy was still in foster care. A meeting with his social worker and the agency's executive director was arranged. I wore my leather jacket for the first time to the meeting. Cleo and Mom were already there. When the meeting began, Cleo was the first to speak.

"I've been informed that you checked my employment and my brother's employment and school records."

The agency's executive director, Charlotte Rosen, was a thin, redheaded woman with thick eyebrows. She showed no emotions as Cleo spoke.

Cleo continued, "When Timothy was placed in foster care,

the goal was to return him to his family after certain conditions were met."

Miss Rosen glanced at her notes. "Miss Powell, that is still the goal."

"Well," Cleo continued, locking eyes with Miss Rosen, "we have complied with your requests. We visit Timothy regularly. We have secured an apartment in a different area. I work. My brother works and attends school. Our mother has started working again. Family Court has granted me custody, yet we have no date for his return."

Sitting across from Cleo, the agency's social worker spoke. "Mrs. Powell's attendance at AA and her progress in counseling and parenting classes has been notable. She keeps visitation appointments with Timothy and is always on time."

Mom smiled.

But Miss Rosen continued speaking in a stern tone of voice. "When a child is placed in foster care due to allegations of sexual abuse, Child Welfare has to be especially careful when the goal is to return the child to parent. We received Timothy's medical records, and the allegations were proven to be true. And Mrs. Powell initially denied he had been assaulted."

Mom lowered her eyes.

"Our mother was in denial," I said, "but she came around and told the truth about what happened to Timothy. She is in recovery, and she assisted the police. She gave them information that helped capture Charles Wilkinson."

"The Bureau has strict regulations to ensure that children are protected," Miss Rosen replied.

"Charles Wilkinson is in jail," I responded.

Cleo gave me an encouraging glance.

"There were other concerns," Miss Rosen continued. She opened the folder in front of her.

Cleo shifted in her seat.

Miss Rosen glanced at several pages. "Timothy's school records were checked. His attendance was poor, and it was reported that he often had colds."

Cleo and I looked at Mom, who appeared stunned. But she quickly regained her composure. "I made mistakes in raising my son, but that's the past, and I will not be tied to it."

Cleo smiled. I gave Mom an approving nod.

Miss Rosen continued. "Timothy was underweight when he entered foster care, but now—"

"We know the Harrington's take excellent care of him," Cleo interrupted, "and that he has gained weight and grown taller."

I shook my head in agreement. "When will Timothy be released from foster care?"

"Mr. Powell, it will be a gradual process. First, there will be weekend visits. And when we see how that goes, he will be officially discharged."

"I'm ready to forego my trip at the end of June and have Timothy start weekend visits," Cleo said quickly.

I was surprised that Cleo was willing to make such a sacrifice. I knew how important the trip with Michael was to her. Miss Rosen referred to the folder.

"Timothy receives weekly counseling and speech therapy. Arrangements must be made for continuation of services near your new address. That will take time. I know the family," she said, giving us an apologetic glance, "is anxious to have Timothy returned, but, Miss Powell, there is no need for you to postpone your trip. I don't foresee Timmy beginning visitations until late August at the earliest."

We left the meeting and rode the elevator in silence. Mom rushed to attend an AA meeting. I hailed a taxi for Cleo, who gave me a hasty hug.

"Call me when you get in," she said.

The cab pulled away. Rush hour was underway, but I got a seat on the train. The noise and crowd only added to my sadness. I had spoken to Chuck Graves the previous Saturday, telling him

I was moving and asking him to transfer me to a store near our new place.

"Will you work full time after graduation?"

My goal was to write full time and work part time, but perhaps I would have to work full time.

Cleo had spoken to me about living in Manhattan.

"Things cost more," she said. "A container of milk is fifty cents. It costs a dollar to get a skirt cleaned."

In the projects, we didn't pay light or gas bills. When we moved, we would. And I saw how fashionable folks were in the city. I needed new clothing.

"Chuck," I said, "it's likely that I'll work full time."

Drizzle was falling when I exited the train at Julius Street in Brownsville. I walked by several guys standing on the corner. Smoking, they seemed oblivious to the weather. I instantly recognized Cool as I hurried across the street, hunched against what had suddenly become a heavy rain. Things had turned sour between Cool and I when I'd refused his request for money.

"There goes smart boy," he said, sneering.

One of his sidekicks slapped him five.

"He's a drip."

I ignored their comments and loud laughter and kept walking.

Once inside our apartment, I had just taken off my wet jacket when the phone rang.

"Hello, handsome," Aunt Rosa said in a raspy voice.

"Hi, Auntie."

"Glad you home 'cause I is about to bring over food."

It was a ritual. She cooked fish and chips every Friday and brought a platter to our door. She sometimes included coleslaw, corn on the cob, and fresh baked apple or peach pie.

"I just got in. Mom is at AA. She left after the meeting about Timothy."

"He coming home soon?"

"We are working on it," I said and sighed.

I suddenly remembered that Cleo had asked me to call her as soon as I got home.

"Aunt Rosa, I've got to make a phone call."

"Okay, I'll bring the food over in a few minutes."

"Good."

Chapter Seven
What's Going On?

Cleo picked up on the first ring.

"Hi, Buddy."

"What's going on?"

"I didn't expect to hear what I heard this afternoon."

"Yeah, I was rocked, too, but I know Timothy will come back to us."

"Buddy, how is Ma?"

I was startled. She sounded so serious.

"What do you mean?"

"I know she's working again and attending counseling, parenting classes, and AA meetings, but what else does she do?"

"Yeah, she's into all that. But why do you want to know her schedule?"

"I'll get to the point."

"Please do," I said hastily. I knew Aunt Rosa would be knocking any minute.

"The last time I was over, she got several calls."

"And?"

"She was whispering and holding the phone close to her ear. I know she was talking to a man."

"Cleo!"

"She got dressed in a hurry and left."

"Mom was probably going to a meeting or something."

"I think she was going to hang out."

"Are you sure?"

"Well, she pulled her hair from her face and put on high heels and perfume."

"Mom is moving on, Cleo. Didn't you hear her say today that negative stuff was all in the past?"

"But there's more, Buddy!"

"What else?" I asked, getting annoyed.

"Do you drink beer?"

I groaned. "I know about the beer. I saw it, too. It's still in the fridge, unopened."

About two weeks before, I had found a six-pack that Mom had hidden in the fridge's vegetable bin. I gave her the benefit of the doubt, figuring she'd purchased it in a weak moment, but I watched it. I checked it daily to make sure it was there. As of this morning, it was.

"I've got to get off the phone. Aunt Rosa is on her way over with my dinner."

"Oh, so you're brushing me off."

"Hold up! Chill! Mom has changed."

I thought about how she'd once spoke loudly and slapped garish makeup on her wide, dark face. The gooey colors crept into the folds of her eyelids and the creases on her neck. But these days she listened more than she talked. Only a smidgen of dark brown powder covered her face. There was just a hint of lipstick on her lips.

"Give her a break," I said with compassion.

I was so hungry that my head was aching, but I didn't want to leave Cleo angry.

"Hey," I said, "I'll come over tomorrow, and we can hang out. Take me to the place where you ordered that food the time I visited you."

"Does that mean I'm paying?" she said and giggled. I could tell her mood was softening.

I chuckled. I was so relieved to hear the change in her tone.

"Only Sister, tomorrow is payday. My pockets are going to be heavy. I'll treat you."

I heard a sharp knock on the door, so I said, "That's Aunt Rosa, I'll see you tomorrow."

"Bet."

I heard the knocking get even harder.

"Coming," I yelled as my mouth started watering.

I opened the door, but I was surprised to see a Negro man wearing a striking red tie and navy blue jacket standing there.

"Hello! You must be Buddy? Benson?" His voice was a rich baritone. He had a broad smile with even teeth, and his handshake was firm.

"Sir," I stammered.

"What happened?" I thought. "Why was a plainclothes detective at our door?"

I examined the tall, smooth, brown man from head to toe.

"A detective could not afford his vines," I thought.

As my eyes lingered on his neat, close-cut hair, something about him seemed vaguely familiar.

"My, my, my! You certainly grew into a fine-looking young man, Buddy."

"You know me?"

"Know you?" he asked. The chuckle emerging from his broad chest became infectious. "Buddy, you don't recognize me?"

"Sir, I'm trying to recall. Are you from the police station?"

"Police? Oh no! May I come in?"

But before I could respond, he stepped in and closed the door.

"Buddy," he said, "I'm Mr. Robby. James Robby."

"What! Why are you here?"

"I've being seeing your mama. She hasn't told you?"

I thought of the discussion I'd just had with Cleo.

"When did you—"

But before I could finish, I heard another hard knock. I

motioned for Mr. Robby to sit. Aunt Rosa was at the door, holding a large platter covered with aluminum foil.

"Sorry it took me so long. Hazel called. That woman can talk. I finally told her to just come on over so I could get off the phone."

I stared at her.

"There's plenty fish, fries, and slices of apple pie," she said.

I couldn't speak.

"You okay? You look like you seen a ghost."

I mumbled something incoherent, took the food, and hurriedly closed the door.

Mr. Robby had taken a seat. His self-confidence was unmistakable. He had placed his right leg casually across his left knee. I noticed neatly pressed, dark gray, expensive-looking pants, black socks, and polished loafers that probably cost more than I earned in a month.

I wanted to know when he'd started seeing Mom.

I stared at him, and he shifted slightly. For a while, I did not speak. He seemed to notice my apprehension and said, "I thought Mae would be here."

He was the only person I could remember who had ever called my mother Mae. He said her name slowly, elongating the single syllable into a softly flowing, Southern sound. I was too distressed to respond.

"Mae hasn't told you about us?"

I couldn't believe my ears. "Mom ... my family ... has been dealing with some personal stuff," I said briskly.

Mr. Robby uncrossed his legs. "I know. I was at the hospital the night Timothy was admitted."

I was too taken aback to respond.

"My partner and I had just picked up a body from Kings County's morgue when I saw Mae leaving the emergency room."

He reached in his jacket pocket, pulled out a business card, and handed it to me.

Robby & Robinson Funeral Home, Inc.
7036 Lincoln Avenue
Mount Vernon, New York 10550
Tel: 914-MO 8-1985

"I was so surprised to see her," he continued. "I thought Mae was in Chicago. I never dreamed I would see her in Brooklyn. I went with her to the 73 precinct, waited while the cops talked to her, and drove her home. We've been seeing each other ever since. Today, I went to pick her up at AA, like I always do on Fridays. I waited and waited. When she didn't come out, I came here."

I heard him, but the word "Chicago" whirled in my head. I started to remember what I had witnessed that time Daddy had gone shopping.

"You promised to take Mom to Chicago while you had your goddamn hand under her dress!" I shouted.

Mr. Robby's face seemed to crumble. For a long time, he didn't speak. Finally, in a voice low and heavy with repentance, he said, "Buddy, I'm not proud of what I did. What Mae and I did. I lost my wife and children. I suffered."

The man sitting on my sofa, looking like a model in *Ebony* and smelling like a dandy, had come to our house countless times to ostensibly buy eggs. I'd seen him on our porch, drinking my Mom's fresh lemonade. I'd looked forward to his visits. My father's back wasn't strong. He didn't lift me and throw me high and catch me like Mr. Robby did. But Daddy gave me castor oil in the spring, walked with me to herd cows, encouraged me to study, and tucked me in bed.

Living had been hard. I'd watched Daddy stop in the middle of the field with the sun beating down like bullets from warplanes and pull his ancient, faded handkerchief from the pocket of his shapeless bib overalls to wipe perspiration from a dirt-creased brow. He didn't catch the sweat before it ran into his eyes and streamed down his face.

"I declare. It's hot, Buddy," he'd said.

I would nod and keep on chopping or picking. But I would suddenly feel a soft tap on my shoulder. Turning, I would see Daddy, and he'd hand me a large mason jar of ice water that Mom had wrapped in old newspapers to keep cool for us to take to the fields. I would take a few swallows and quickly give the frosted jar back to him. I'd watch his Adam's apple move swiftly up and down as he gulped water. Afterward, he'd stand for a while, looking around before wiping his mouth and mopping his face.

Then he'd quietly say, "Let's go on, son."

Mr. Robby was the man who'd played games with me and brought me candy. He had tickled me under my ribs to make me laugh.

I shouted, "You lowlife! You are a dog! How many times did you fuck Mama in my daddy's house when he was away?"

Mr. Robby squirmed on the sofa.

"Bastard!" I yelled, lunging for him.

Surprisingly, he was a swift, big man who avoided my grasp as he hastily headed for the door.

"I'll return when Mae is home, Buddy. Maybe you and I can talk man-to-man."

Unleashed tears started pouring down my face.

"You fuck!" I screamed, seizing Aunt Rosa's food from the coffee table and hurling the entire platter at him.

He opened the door. Pieces of fish, apple pie, and French fries hit Mom's face, spilling down the front of her jacket.

"Mae! Mae!" Mr. Robby repeated, sounding like a bleating sheep.

"Mom! Mom! Mom!" I yelled, not sounding much better myself.

She dropped her purse and lifted the edge of her jacket to wipe food from her eyelashes.

"Go get something to clean her up with," Mr. Robby said, touching my arm.

I hurried to the bathroom, grabbed a towel, and sprinted back, only to discover Aunt Rosa, Miss Hazel, and Mr. Robby had gathered around Mom.

"We heard the yelling and rushed over," Miss Hazel said. She headed to the kitchen for the broom and dustpan.

"My cooking must have been bad." Aunt Rosa attempted to make a joke, but the concern was visible on her face. I wondered what she would think when she found out what had really happened.

Mr. Robby removed Mom's jacket and guided her to the sofa. Her stockings were stained, and her shoes were splattered. Her green jacket was spotted with grease.

"Mae, are you all right? You didn't get cut or anything?"

"I am all right! But what is going on?" She was suddenly aware of all the faces staring at her. "I don't know what's going on, but I'm not going to forget my manners. Rosa, Hazel, this here is James Robby. I know him from when we lived Down South."

I gathered my jacket and book bag from the kitchen table and headed for the door.

"Buddy! Where you going?" Mother asked sharply. "Ain't you going tell me why you threw that food?"

"Buddy, you threw the food?" Miss Hazel and Aunt Rosa asked in one voice.

Eyes stared at me, and ears waited to hear me speak, but I was unable to talk.

"Mae, I caused it. Honey, I came here 'cause I was waiting there for so long."

"You were there? Where?"

"You know, on Fridays, I'm always at the AA door on Hoyt Street in Brooklyn."

"Rob, you forgot! I told you that after the meeting at the foster care office, I was going to an AA meeting in the city."

"I did forget, and look at the mess my forgetting caused."

"Buddy, I think you need to explain!" Mom said quickly.

"I ... I ... I," I stammered.

But Aunt Rosa promptly said, "Hazel, let's go so they can talk."

Then, just as she and Miss Hazel reached the door, it opened. Rita Ann stepped in.

"Mother, I knew I would find you here."

"Me and Rosa were just leaving. You all dressed up. Where you going?"

"Jay is waiting downstairs. We are going to celebrate."

"What you celebrating?" Miss Hazel asked apprehensively.

"I passed the school secretary exam. The letter was in the mail when I got home from work. Jay is taking me to dinner and to hear some music."

I rushed over and touched Rita's arm. "Let me catch a ride with you," I said, hoping she'd see the urgency in my eyes.

Without waiting for an answer from her and ignoring the stunned expressions on everyone's faces, I nodded good-bye to Mom and quickly pushed Rita Ann out the door, past Aunt Rosa and Miss Hazel. I sprinted toward the elevator.

Chapter Eight
Into the City

Jay's old deuce and a quarter was long and low. I crawled into a backseat littered with books and rumpled gym clothes.

"Hey, just push that stuff to the side," he said over the sounds of King Curtis' saxophone. I did. Afterward, I squeezed my eyes shut and rested my head against the window.

"How could things have gotten so upside down and crazy?" I thought. "I did the right thing. I had gotten permission to leave school early so I could visit the agency with Mom and Cleo. And look how those fucking bureaucrats acted!"

Then hearing Cleo talk about postponing her trip was a real shock. My God, seeing Mr. Robby standing at our door was totally unexpected. Cleo's suspicions about our mother seeing someone had been confirmed.

"But why hadn't Mom mentioned something about him?" I thought. "Had he been coming over when I was in school? Did he stop by on Saturday's while I was working? Had Mom purchased the beer for him?"

There had been changes between Mom and me. We'd started communicating. When she worked from four to twelve, we talked and had coffee after I got home from school. On Saturday mornings, she fixed breakfast before I rushed off to the supermarket. I never left the house without hugging her. She told me she loved me more often. Now I wondered if it had been a ploy.

"Was she putting on an act?" I thought, feeling betrayed. "How could she not tell me she had been seeing Mr. Robby?"

After the disappointing news at the agency, the subway ride, and the phone call to Cleo, I just wanted a good meal, a little TV, and some sleep.

"But look what happened!" I thought.

It was funny how things had worked out. Lola was supposed to have been here this weekend, but she had called a few days ago.

* * *

"Buddy?"

Hearing her voice felt great.

"Hi, baby," I said.

"I can't come to see you. I've got to be here. A mock nursing state board exam is scheduled for the last Saturday in May."

I was very disappointed. "I miss you. A lot has been going on here."

"What's happening?"

"I've got five tickets for my graduation exercise. One for Mom, Cleo, Rita Ann, Aunt Rosa, and you."

"I'm so proud of you, Buddy."

I wished I could crawl through the phone and kiss her.

"I met with Mr. Rosenberg and Chuck Graves. I told you about him. Chuck is offering me an assistant manager position at a store on 96th near Broadway. That's not far from our new apartment."

"So you got the apartment? That's good news."

"Yeah. One of Cleo's friends found it for us. It's on Central Park West and 100th Street. You can see the park from the living room. It has two large bedrooms and washers and dryers in the basement. But I ain't jumping up and down about the job offer."

"Why not? It sounds good."

"I'll make more money. God knows we're going to need it. But I don't want to get sucked in."

"What do you mean?"

"Getting that article published encouraged me. I need to concentrate on writing."

"You sound angry."

"I'm not. I'm eager to write, but I'll work full time for awhile."

"When you all moving?"

"Soon. Zelda, the actress who owns the apartment where Cleo has been staying, is returning from a road show."

"How's your mother? How's Cleo?"

"Mom is attending meetings. Cleo is a vegetarian these days."

"What's happening with her and Michael?"

"I speak to him now and then. He and Cleo want to take you and me to a fancy place after the graduation ceremony. Is that okay by you?"

"I'd love it!"

"He sounds like a real nice cat. He and his dad are expanding their real estate firm. He wrote for his college newspaper. He thinks Max Roach is the greatest drummer on Earth."

"You think they're getting serious?"

"I think they're good for each other right now."

"Oh?"

"Cleo will get custody of Timothy, but she's going to make some changes once things straighten out."

"What do you think she's going to do?"

"Well, fixing up the apartment inspired her. She's talking about studying interior decorating, but she's restless."

"Is she reckless?"

"She's not. She's a responsible neurotic, if you can understand that."

"You love her, don't you?"

"Very much so."

"It's good to hear about the move, but Auntie is going to miss you all."

"The move is only the beginning. I'm going to make money and get my piece of the American pie."

"I know what you mean. When I pass the state boards and become a real nurse, I'm going to get an apartment and buy a car."

I smiled. "And you and I are going to hit the road often."

* * *

Now in the backseat of Jay's car, I felt like shit.

"How could I have become so angry and thrown food at someone?" I thought.

I realized what had triggered my reaction. The memory of Mom and Mr. Robby's indiscretion so many years ago had really gotten next to me.

"How could they have carried on in my father's house?" I thought. "How vulgar and foul their behavior had been! How disrespectful and low they had acted!"

I recalled "My Self Face." I had definitely shown my angry self face this evening. And when I thought about Mom keeping her new relationship with Mr. Robby from me, I knew I needed to trust my self face that meditates.

Rita Ann's gentle shake brought me back to the present.

"Buddy, did you fall asleep?"

In the rearview mirror, I saw Jay's huge, hazel eyes examining me.

"You all right, man?" he asked.

My head ached, and I was hungry as hell.

"I'm cool. Where we at?"

"In the Village."

I glanced out the window. I saw a telephone booth on the corner.

"Pull over, man."

I slapped Jay five, kissed Rita Ann's cheek, grabbed my book bag, and quickly hopped out of the car. After sprinting to the phone booth, I hurriedly dialed my number. The line was busy. I dialed Cleo's and got a busy signal, too.

"Cleo and Mom are probably talking," I said aloud.

"How is Mom telling Cleo what happened?" I thought. "What had Mr. Robby told Mom? Did he tell her about our conversation before I threw the food? Had he told Mom what I'd observed so long ago?"

Sex and intimacy were tender topics for me. MaryAlice would jam her bubble gum-tasting tongue in my mouth and bring my hands to her braless chest. Between my legs, a throbbing would start, and my pants couldn't contain the swelling. I'd explored when MaryAlice unzipped my fly and rolled my enlargement between her breasts. When the rumor started that MaryAlice was pregnant, I was stunned, angry, and feeling betrayed. What we did could not make babies. I had never done what needed to be done to make babies.

I wondered if I could ever have a fulfilling relationship. When I thought MaryAlice might have been pregnant, I remembered what I'd witnessed between Mom and Mr. Robby and Mom and the Chinese man, not to mention her other casual relationships. And I realized that those experiences had profoundly affected me. Cleo appeared to have been affected as well. She'd attempted to hide and seek refuge behind a mask, saying she was unconventional, but I knew she was afraid to make serious commitments. She had difficulties trusting others.

Again, I dialed my number. This time, there was no answer. I dialed Cleo, and she picked up on the first ring.

"Hi, Buddy."

"Were you speaking to Mom a little while ago?

"I was talking to her until she left to see Aunt Rosa."

"Did she tell you what happened?"

"What do you mean?

"She didn't tell you what I did?"

"No, she didn't say you did anything, but she said you left with Rita Ann in a hurry."

I looked out the phone booth. Across the street was a subway station.

"Well, I did something, and I need to return home."

"Michael and I are driving to Brooklyn. Mother did tell me something important."

"I'm on Avenue of the Americas and West 4th Street. I'll jump on the train and head home, too."

"Buddy, you're around the corner from Tony's. Michael and I eat there now and then. Grab a Coke, a couple of slices and wait. We'll pick you up."

"Didn't Mom tell you that Mr. Robby was there? When she came home and opened the door, I threw Aunt Rosa's food at him, but the food hit her instead. It spilled down the jacket you gave her. Aunt Rosa and Miss Hazel came to see what all the fuss was about. Rita Ann also came over. I hitched a ride with her and Jay."

"What? My God, she didn't tell me any of that. I understand why you want to go home."

"Well, what did Mom tell you?"

"She's pregnant. She and Mr. Robby are having a baby."

I hung up and took Mr. Robby's card from my pocket. Scattered thoughts ran through my mind.

"Mom is pregnant. Mr. Robby is responsible. How would this affect me and Cleo and, above all, Timothy's release from foster care? Mr. Robby said he lost his wife and children. Were they divorced? Would he marry Mom? Would she want to get married? My God."

I stepped out of the booth and headed across the street.

"What if the platter I had thrown had hit her in the stomach?" I thought.

I hurried past the park where a boisterous crowd was watching a basketball game. Players scored and ran around slapping high fives, chasing and teasing each other like first-graders. Some lit and casually passed cigarettes around like candy. A few ignored the "No Drinking" signs and took generous slugs from large beer bottles while munching on pizza. Others pranced, strutted, and wiped sweat from wet brows. The spectators clapped and shouted encouraging words when their favorite team scored. I couldn't recall the last time I'd laughed, teased, and goofed off with friends, dudes at school, or cats at the supermarket. Glancing at the players, I promised myself that the next time I had the chance to chill, I would.

"Check out the jacket," a nasally voice said.

I was moving fast and thinking hard. I paid no attention to the comment until a familiar voice said, "Well, if it ain't smart boy."

I turned to face Cool and three of his boys.

"Sho is. But who let him out his cage?" His pal with the wide nose asked.

Cool's narrow, black-as-midnight face shone in the fading light.

"How come squares like you hang in the Village?" he asked, sneering.

"Yeah, the Village is for hip people, not punks and squares," one of his sidekicks said.

I wasn't afraid of Cool, but he had his posse. I stared at them and quickly turned to continue walking.

"I bet his pockets is heavy 'cause he got a gig at that big supermarket in Brownsville," the tallest of the three said.

"Yeah, he be working," Cool retorted. "Boy be hustling out early every Saturday morning. I see him from my window."

"Shake him down, Cool," the guy with the nasal voice demanded.

"No, you do that, man. I got something else on my mind."

Up ahead, I could see the flashing green and red sign for Tony's, and I hurried forward. But Cool was suddenly standing in front of me, and his gang had surrounded me.

"Punk!"

"Get out of my way, Cool."

"Whatcha gon' do, asshole?" And he shoved me hard.

I threw up my hands. "Get your rabid pals out of the way, Cool. I will take you on."

"I likes you jacket."

"Cool, you are bad news." I attempted to pass him.

"I said I likes your jacket, motherfucker."

"Country!" the wide, heavy guy yelled. He sprung on his short legs, hit me hard in the chest, and caused me to drop my book bag. "Give him the fucking jacket."

The boldness of his move surprised me, but I wasn't shaken. But, when Cool started viciously kicking my bag, I said sharply, "Cut your shit, Cool."

His rage-filled face looked as if it would explode. He raised a fist.

"This is the last time I is going to tell you. I like the jacket your ass is wearing, and I want the motherfucking jacket!"

"You sorry excuse for a human, I'm not giving you shit." I bent to retrieve my book bag.

Cool's sharp toe shoe landed deep in my rear. I lost my balance and fell hard to the curb.

"Shit." I jumped to my feet, grabbed Cool by his collar, and lifted him off the ground.

"You ... you ... you," I searched for words.

Cool reached in his back pocket. A silver object was suddenly visible.

"Fuck," he said.

He struck my jaw with the shiny item. It was the same sensation I felt when I had broken my arm. I reached for my jaw, and I was knocked to the ground. My head landed on my book bag, and I was surprised to see a sticky red covering it. Hard shoes stomped my neck and head, but I grabbed a pair of ankles. My hands were crimson and sticky. I realized the gummy fluid was blood … my blood. The silver flash in Cool's hand had been a knife.

A hard shoe pressed my head deep into the book bag as Cool jabbed at my arms and chest with the knife. In horror, I saw more shoes lifting and kicking me. But a worn pair of brogans remained anchored. A large knapsack dropped, and books, flyers, and peanuts fell out, landing near my head.

"Get off him!"

"Run! Run!"

Strong, rough hands lifted me. My head came to rest in overweight arms. My vision was blurred, and breathing was painful, but I smelled peppermint and knew I was in the grasp of Earl Ernest Johnson. He leaned in close, and his bushy hair brushed my jaw.

"Hang in there, Brother Buddy."

I heard screeching tires and then rapid steps. Black low-heeled boots were standing close to my head.

"Buddy! Buddy!" Cleo screamed.

A white male's hand reached to take my pulse.

Someone yelled, "Call an ambulance!"

My jaw throbbed. Blood poured from cuts in my arms and chest. Earl Ernest's once-white shirt was now smudged red. Cleo's hair fell in my face as she bent to kiss me. Michael's warm hand stroked my rapidly cooling face. I closed my eyes and fell into a bottomless sleep.

Chapter Nine
Rushing

I was in a bright passage. Images flashed through my mind as I rushed upward. I saw myself in the house Down South, crawling, tugging a tablecloth, and sending plates and silverware crashing to the floor. Later, I was in a round tin tub, splashing and reaching for a floating, bright yellow, red-beaked plastic duck. I saw Mom holding my hands as I took my first steps. Images of our dog, me, Cleo, the twins, Mickey and Mildred, flooded my mind.

Up ahead, I saw a door. I knew that if I opened it, I would no longer be in pain. I reached for the knob but I heard Daddy saying, "No, Benson it's not your time."

I was happy to know he was on the other side.

"I want to be with you. I miss you," I said. " Over there, I will suffer no more."

"Not yet, Buddy."

"Daddy, I don't want to go on."

"Talk to me, son."

"Daddy, so much has gone wrong. After you died, we were thrown off the farm and given one-way tickets to New York, but I saw none of the good living that folks talked about."

"I'm listening, Buddy."

"All kinds of stuff went on with Mom and us. It hurts to talk about it."

"Time heals, Buddy."

"But I'm always struggling. School was wrenching. I was so ashamed. I was in the third grade and could scarcely read. Miss Griffin helped me. She was the best teacher. I was going to graduate from high school in a few weeks, the first male in our family to do so, but look where I am."

"Buddy, all is not lost."

"Ha, that's easy for you to say."

"Things will work out in a while, son."

"Yeah, well how much more time will it take? Mom hasn't been honest. You remember Mr. Robby, Dad? She was carrying on with him when you were alive!"

"I've forgiven Clara Mae."

"But I found out Mom has been seeing Mr. Robby again. He even came to our door. I threw a platter of food at him, but the food hit Mom instead. I rushed out the house and hitched a ride. A group of fools attacked me. That's how I got here, and now I'm dying."

"Your mother is still young, and it isn't your time to die."

"Daddy, that's not all. Mom had been seeing a real loser who sexually assaulted Timothy, and he was taken away from us and placed in foster care."

"Buddy, good can come from the worst tragedies."

"You may be right. Mom started attending AA and taking parenting classes. She stopped wearing tight clothing. She stopped smoking, too. She seems to be on the right track. Cleo works hard. She has a guy who is taking her to Europe, and she isn't as self-centered. I was offered an assistant manager position at the supermarket where I work. I give Mom money, and I've saved money, too. I hoped to buy my yearbook and class ring. I believed things were turning around. We got an apartment in a nice area. We were working on getting Timothy back with us. But, Daddy, right before I was assaulted, Cleo told me that Mom is pregnant. She and Mr. Robby are going to have a baby."

"She deserves a chance at getting things right, Buddy. It sounds like she's straightened up."

"Well, I'm angry, and I feel betrayed! What's going to happen with Timothy now?"

"Have faith, son."

"Daddy, you don't understand."

"Yes, I do. Everything you've told me, I already knew. Remember the hymn, 'You Will Understand It Better By and By?' Buddy, you are being prepared for the places you will go and the things you will do."

"But, Daddy, I'm always worried."

"You will do more than you've ever imagined."

"You sound so sure."

"What's been getting you through? What have you been holding on to, son?"

"My dreams, Daddy. They have kept me going, but now I'm crossing over."

"Buddy, you will not die. Take your hand off the knob! Turn around now!"

I opened my eyes. Cleo gasped and gestured toward Michael. He and the paramedic rushed over. Through the oxygen mask, I attempted to speak. I wanted to tell them how I almost crossed over to be with Daddy. But I started coughing blood. Michael wiped my lips.

His blue eyes never left my face while the paramedic took my blood pressure and the ambulance's sirens wailed on its way to the hospital.

Chapter Ten
Recovery

"At least taste the oatmeal, Buddy. It's got cinnamon on top. Mr. Robby didn't mind dropping me off. It's a short trip from Mt. Vernon," Mom said.

Mom had moved out of the projects. She was now living with Mr. Robby, and she took advantage of the hospital's unrestricted visiting hours. Cool's crude weapon had broken my jawbone, damaged the olfactory nerve, ripped back muscles, and torn the rotator cuffs in both arms. Morphine was constantly administered to ease my pain. I began to enjoy how ecstatic and free it made me feel and eagerly looked forward to the next dose. I would sweat and become anxious if the injections were late.

Michael's cousin, a doctor, knew someone who knew someone. In July, I was transferred from Beth Israel in New York City to a private infirmary and rehabilitation center in White Plains, Westchester. Now, in the middle of August, I was convalescing, attending physical therapy, and trying to regain arm motion. I was also receiving counseling.

I looked at Mom's expanding middle. "Aren't you and Mr. Robby going shopping for baby furniture today?"

"That's much later. I've got plenty of time to spend with you."

I groaned and glanced at the electric typewriter, a gift from Cleo and Michael. I had planned to write before my session in the pool with the physical therapist. Just then, Miss Vivian, the kitchen aide, a baked potato brown, tall, heavy-set, moon-faced woman who was about Mom's age, strolled in. Her gold-and-white uniform was immaculate, and her white shoes were spotless. On her face was concern when she saw my half-eaten breakfast.

"Buddy, the food wasn't good?"

Actually, the cooking at the place was excellent. I'd eaten foods that were unfamiliar, including, endive, cauliflower, baked ziti, penne, eggplant, garlic Rosemary bread, and kiwi.

Before I could respond, Mom spoke, "Miss Vivian, I tried to get him to eat. He's getting better, but he needs to put on weight."

She nodded. "Miss Mae, by the time Buddy is discharged, he will have picked up. I'll help see to that."

Mom and Miss Vivian continued chatting about food and cooking, but my mind wandered. I thought of Earl Ernest. He had been handing out leaflets and trying to raise the consciousness of brothers. He had saved my life that night in May. But the truth was chilling. Brothers had savagely attacked and almost killed me.

* * *

"Your attackers have been apprehended," Earl Ernest said after he had mercilessly beaten me at a game of chess during a recent visit. "They were caught breaking and entering an apartment in the Village on West 4th Street."

I started perspiring. Hearing that Cool and his thugs had been captured was a relief, but I hoped I wouldn't have to testify. I didn't want to relive the horror. I thought about what that louse, Charles, had done to Timothy, and I wondered how such creeps could live with themselves.

"Earl, when you become an attorney, would you defend folks like Cool and his boys?"

"That's a tough question, brother."

"Every brother ain't a brother, Earl Ernest."

"Yeah, but every brother is a person."

I leaned back. "It seems to me that some persons are more personable than others."

Earl scrutinized me, put a peppermint in his mouth, and quietly said, "Buddy, everybody has a story. Most times, many lines add up to some unrighteous chapters. But after the whole book is written, the account may not be so harsh."

"Earl, I think men like Andy Young, James Meredith, and James Farmer are brothers."

"I am sorry about what happened to you, Buddy. You didn't deserve it. Cool and his gang should and will be punished, but don't be so self-righteous."

I stared at him, but I was recalling words my father spoke when I had almost crossed over. "Good can come from tragedies."

Suddenly, I started thinking about the kid everyone called Cool. "How many people remembered that Jerome Lewis was his real name or that he and I had attended the same elementary school?"

He'd been in a higher grade and sat in the rear of the auditorium on assembly days when students were required to wear white shirts and blouses. But it was hard to tell the color of Cool's grimy shirt. He always managed to have an aisle seat where he stuck out his feet to trip smaller children. He threw spitballs at teachers and made hooting sounds at performers. He lived somewhere in the housing projects, but I didn't know where or who with. He always had a pack of Kool cigarettes peeking out his rear pants pockets. He appeared to be laid back and calm, thus the nickname.

I wondered if he had ever visited the library or played basketball. I wondered what his favorite television program was. In spite of myself, my eyes began to water.

Busily putting away the chess pieces, Earl paused to look at me.

"Buddy, you all right?"

"I was thinking that Cool has had it tough."

"He's probably in a lot of pain, and doesn't know how to handle it. You understand?"

I did. I realized that writing had helped me cope with my suffering, anguish, and pain. Writing had helped my living easier to live, but I wondered what could have helped Cool.

Finally, I said, "Man, you know Cool is somebody's child."

"That he is, Brother Buddy. That he is."

* * *

"Buddy! Buddy!" Mom touched my arm, which brought me back to the present. "Miss Vivian told me they got salmon, garlic roasted potatoes, string beans, and strawberry shortcake for lunch."

"That sounds good."

"Make sure you eat plenty and, if necessary, ask for seconds," she whispered as she gathered her purse.

She walked toward the door, but turned quickly. "I'm coming back with Mr. Robby tonight. I have something for you, and we need to talk with you."

I nodded and glanced at my watch. Realizing I had fifteen minutes to get to the pool, I hurriedly prepared to leave.

The session with my physical therapist had motivated my appetite, and I ate lunch greedily. I was still hungry, but I was too embarrassed to ask for more. I searched through the foodstuff that Chuck Graves and Mr. Rosenberg left earlier in the week. I grabbed a box of cookies and started working.

As I edited "Inside Toilet," my father's words ran through my mind. "You will do more than you ever imagine."

I'd been at it for a while. I needed a break and rose to visit Mr. Logan, a charismatic, retired history professor recuperating from a stroke. He had introduced me to Herman Melville, Henry David Thoreau, Dante, and chess. Then I remembered Mom was returning and sat back down. I supposed she wanted to talk about Timothy's pending release from foster care, but I wondered why she was coming with Mr. Robby and not Cleo.

I heard the clamor of the food cart, and I prepared for dinner. I was eating and watching the news. President Johnson was talking about increasing troops in South Vietnam when the phone rang.

"Buddy!" Timothy's voice resounded in my ear.

"Timothy, it's good to hear you."

His social worker thought it was too traumatic for him to visit. I disagreed and voiced my objections through Mom and Cleo, but he called almost daily.

"Buddy, did you get my last get-well card?" Before I could answer, he said excitedly, "I put one of my drawings in it, too."

I had posted his cards and drawings around my room, including fat, smiling bears jumping on yellow trapezes, brown boys pulling wagons loaded with green balls, white kids riding red and blue bicycles. The colorful genre paintings reminded me of Horace Pippin.

Now I glanced at Timothy's latest illustration, a calico cat with a bright orange collar that had a gold bell. The cat's front paw rested on a ball. Over its head was a beaming yellow sun. In the background, tall trees enclosed a house with blue curtains.

"I got it, Timothy. Boy, you are some artist."

He laughed. "Cleo brought me more paints, colored pencils, and drawing paper. You know what my favorite color is?"

"Isn't it the whole rainbow?"

"No, silly. I like blue."

"Oh."

"Know what my favorite day is?"

"No, tell me."

"It's the day I'm going see you," he said, his laughter growing louder.

"Timothy, when will that be?"

"Can you keep a secret?"

"Of course. I'm your brother."

"I overheard Mrs. Harrington, Cleo, and Mom talking. You'll see me in September 'cause I'm going to start having overnight and weekend visits."

"Oh, Timothy," I said. My voice was cracking. "It's too good to be true!"

He squealed when I told him the new apartment faced Central Park and the Museum of National History was nearby. He was excited when I told him that I would take him there.

"When, Buddy?"

I sighed. "I'm not sure."

"Mom and Cleo said you were eating more and swimming every day, so I bet you'll be home real soon."

My appetite was improving. Movement in my arms and shoulders was stronger. I no longer craved drugs. In biweekly sessions, I met with Matt, my psychologist.

"I'm dealing with a lot right now."

"You still mad 'cause they wouldn't let me visit you?"

His candor took me aback. "I'm annoyed about that and some other things, too."

"I talk with my social worker about stuff that gets me upset."

"You do?"

"Yeah."

"What do you talk about?"

"Well, I talk about what happened with Charles."

I didn't respond.

"I talk about how you were attacked and how I feel about leaving Mrs. Harrington."

"Do you feel better after you talk?" I asked cautiously.

"Yeah. I'm getting better."

Working with Matt had helped me, too. I was less depressed and having fewer nightmares. I had even apologized to Mom and Mr. Robby. But I still carried a residual anger. Mr. Robby had disrespected my father, our home, his wife, and his children. Mom should have told me she was seeing him again. I felt betrayed.

* * *

Matt said, "Buddy, there is no question that gratuitous, agonizing, and distressing things have happened to you. It's obvious your mother disappointed you, but perhaps she did the best she could."

I didn't respond.

"Buddy, you are still very angry."

For the first time, I made the connection. Pain and anger were alike. I recalled what I had witnessed through the window of our house, my struggles to do well in school, the shame of living in the projects, the experience with Timothy and Charles, and how awful I felt when Cleo told me she was postponing her trip to Europe until I was discharged from the hospital. I knew how important that trip with Michael had been to her.

I yelled and said to Matt, "I keep asking, 'Why me?' What did I do to deserve all this pain? I've tried to do right all my life!"

In a voice as soothing as warm milk, Matt said, "Life and living can often be unfair, Buddy."

* * *

Now I said softly, "Many things happened to me, you, and our family. Living has not been easy for us."

Timothy sighed. "Buddy, remember when Mrs. Harrington

would bring me to the office for visits and you would give me Tootsie Rolls and read me your Furious Red stories?

"I do."

"I said I was on a break."

"You said that?"

"Yes, Buddy."

I suddenly recalled my father's words. "Things will work out in a while, son."

I took a deep breath. "You're right, Timothy. And the rest of your life is only going to be better."

* * *

Talking with Timothy left me feeling rattled. I wouldn't be there to help with his return home. Cleo had organized the move into the new apartment.

"I only had clothing, books, and records. Michael and Jill helped me," she said when I mentioned how awful I felt about not being able to assist.

"Cleo, you've really been at it. You helped Mr. Robby move Mom out the projects, too."

"Jay, Rita Ann, Aunt Rosa, and Miss Hazel pitched in, too."

"You're decorating the new place?"

"Yes. It's fun. I bet I could make money at it."

Cleo once said she planned to study interior decorating, but she was impulsive and lost interest quickly. Now she sounded convincing, so I kept quiet.

"Charlotte Rosen approved a furniture allowance for five hundred dollars," she continued. "I purchased twin beds, a lamp, and a throw rug for the room you and Timothy will share."

"You'll need to buy other things," I murmured.

I opened the bedside table. I grabbed several bills from my

tobacco can and handed them to her. She tucked the money in her leather bag without counting it.

"Thanks," she said. "The money will help, but I've been finding stuff left on the streets around Central Park West and West End Avenue. I picked up a round oak kitchen table plus two stools. Last week, I found a white leather sofa. It just needed a good cleaning 'cause it smelled like cat urine."

"Is that legal? Can you go through trash without getting in trouble?"

She looked at me in amazement. "It's not garbage picking. It's furniture hunting. It's a chic, West Side thing done with style and flair. Even Jill does it, and she can afford to buy whatever she wants."

"How do you get the stuff home?"

"On the night before bulk trash day, folks put goodies out. Then Michael and I go searching. When we find something worthwhile, we put it in his car. But Michael's MG is small. A couple of times, we had to flag a taxi."

I didn't know what to say.

"I've used money I'd saved for my trip for dishes, silverware, pots, and pans. I don't want secondhand cooking utensils."

I felt sad. Cleo had diligently saved for the trip to Europe with Michael. I needed to make some money.

"You said that living in Manhattan is expensive. As soon as I get out of here, I'll start that assistant manager position."

"You worry too much." She nodded toward the typewriter. "How's your writing coming along?"

"I've submitted two short stories, and one was accepted for publication."

"Well," she said, smiling, "I think you can forget about working in the supermarket, Older Brother."

I watched as she headed to the visitor's restroom. She had come straight from work and looked very professional in a lime green chemise dress. The seams of her off-black stockings were perfectly straight, and her high heels were stunning.

Dinner was being served.

"Stay," I offered.

"Not this time," she said, gathering her purse. "I promised Mom I'd stop by when I left here."

"Does she live in a nice place?"

"I think so. The house is near the hospital where Mom's doctors are. It's got three bedrooms and a backyard."

"Mr. Robby is doing all right by her?"

"From what I can tell, things seem fine. He takes her to medical appointments and AA meetings. He seems okay."

"Maybe they should get married," I said. "They started carrying on when we were living Down South."

Cleo gazed at me and sighed. "Buddy, they're adults. Try letting go of the past."

I again recalled my father's words. "I've forgiven Clara Mae."

I realized my remark was insensitive.

"Live in the present, Buddy. It's a lot less stressful." She blew me a kiss and left.

* * *

Now a soft rain had started. I watched ducks swimming lazily on the slow, breeze-rippling pond and reflected on my life. I opened the tobacco can and pulled out the remaining crumbled bills, totaling two hundred and eleven dollars. Timothy's favorite color was blue. I imagined how we could have shopped for a blue bedspread and colorful sheets and pillowcases.

And for the umpteenth time, I asked, "Why? Why have I experienced so much pain?"

I wondered what it would have been like if I had lived in the suburbs with both parents in a nice home filled with books and music. But perhaps my disheveled life was a blessing of sorts. It had motivated me to write.

I suddenly thought of Lola. She commuted from Baltimore weekly, and I cherished her visits. The crisis with Timothy, her studying, and my attack hadn't allowed us to date. Here, we got to know each other, and my feelings for her intensified.

The last time she visited, she looked good in a white and blue, belted shirtwaist dress. I embraced her and started to bury my nose in her hair when I saw that her once-cascading waves, the ones I loved to touch and smell, now stopped around her earlobes.

"Why did you get it cut?" I asked.

"I wanted a more mature appearance."

She was gracious when Mr. Logan dropped off a book he had promised to lend me, but I couldn't wait for him to leave. Lunch arrived, and she placed the food on the table by the window. The flowers she had brought were placed in a large vase. The lamb chops, sautéed vegetables, and mashed garlic potatoes were delicious, but I only nibbled as Lola spoke of job interviews, salaries, and such.

"I want to work in a hospital connected with a medical college 'cause the pay is better," she said between sips of tea.

I squeezed her hand. I knew how much she wanted a car and a place to call her own.

"Where have you been looking?"

"I've interviewed at Johns Hopkins Hospital, but I'm not limiting myself to Baltimore."

"What other places have you checked out?"

"My youngest brother and Dad are in Charleston, South Carolina. I sent my résumé there, but the West Coast appeals to me, too."

"That's so far away."

She smiled. "I'll go any place that pays well."

"Lola, you're special. You're together." I attempted to kiss her neck, but she pulled away.

"I'm being too forward," I thought.

To cool down, I showed her my diploma that Cleo had picked up, along with the school ring and yearbook that Mom had purchased as a surprise.

"It's only a beginning, Buddy."

I stared at her. I hadn't expected that response. It seemed so indifferent. In the silence, we looked out the window.

She finally said, "Buddy, when I met you, I liked you 'cause you were tall and good-looking, but I started liking other things, too. You called when you said you would, you listened to me, and I liked the way you had been there for your brother."

I turned to gaze at her, but I read nothing in her eyes.

"I knew you were special."

"Girl, when I first saw you, my heart jumped. I liked your style and the way you looked."

I reached for her, but she stiffened.

"Baby, what's wrong?"

"Buddy," she whispered, "I think you want more from me and our relationship than I'm able to give."

Stunned, I asked, "What does that mean?"

"It means I'm finally able to take care of me and get some of the things I want. I can give something to Aunt Rosa, too."

"So it's about money? You know I'm going to be an assistant manager when I get out of here. I'll be able to give you what you need."

She turned from me to gaze out the window. The ducks had disappeared, and the pond appeared desolate.

"We both know you're not going to take that job."

I didn't respond.

"What would you be doing today if I hadn't arrived?"

"I would be working, editing a story that's been accepted for publication."

"Honey, writing is your passion."

"Right, Lola, but I want material things, too. I want a car, clothing, and maybe a house. You know how much I like you. I hoped you and I could be together and we'd enjoy the simple things until the bucks come."

"Like what?"

"A slow day at the beach. Walking in the park. A picnic. An evening playing chess, reading, and just talking."

Once again, Daddy's words came to me. "Things will work out in a while, son."

She studied me for a minute. "Buddy, are you the next James Baldwin?"

I glanced at the pile of manuscripts and revisions on the table near the typewriter.

"No, I'm the first Benson Lee Powell Jr."

*　*　*

The floodlights switched on, illuminating the ducks. They resembled bits of floating alabaster. The rain had made the shrubbery glisten, and everything was quiet. I heard someone suddenly clear a throat, and I turned to see Mom and Mr. Robby.

Whenever I saw Mr. Robby, my feelings alternated between forgiveness and anger. Now he was in my room, towering over my mother, whose protruding middle caused her to lean back. In his left hand, he held the battered suitcase in which I had packed my possessions when we left the South. His right arm was draped gently and protectively around Mom's shoulder.

They looked at me. Their staid formal appearance caused a swelling in my throat, and I slowly rose and cautiously started walking toward them. With each step, I felt as if I were letting go of a burdensome and strained past and the weight of an unforgiving spirit.

I moved carefully. My eyes never left their faces. The closer I came, the more the hard feelings I held for Mr. Robby felt like they were slipping away. I stood before the two of them, and I was crying so hard that I couldn't speak. Mr. Robby's big face appeared as jagged as broken glass. He was overcome with emotion, and Mom was sobbing as she took the suitcase from Mr. Robby.

"Buddy, I found this when we were packing to move, and I thought you'd want it."

I recalled how I had hastily stuffed family photos, my first book of Furious Red stories, and my meager clothing in the valise the day we were tossed out of our house Down South. I thought about the struggles we had gone through up north and how difficult life and living had been for us, and I cried harder.

I wanted the valise. It would remind me of how far my family and I had come and how our love had kept us from going under.

I reached to hug Mom, but Mr. Robby grabbed me and nodded to Mom. "Buddy, we have something to tell you."

"What is it?"

He hesitated for an instant and cleared his throat. "Your mother and me ... well, we're getting married. We want you to be the best man."

Epilogue

It's Christmas Eve 1968. On the radio, the Drifters are singing "I'm Dreaming of a White Christmas." In a short while, I will hail a taxi to Grand Central Station and board the 4:45 Metro North train for the twenty-five-minute ride to Mount Vernon.

Timothy called earlier to tell me that Mom was preparing roasted turkey, potato salad, corn bread, collard greens, and sweet potatoes. I'm excited about being with my family. We laugh and talk together, and Mom has become an outstanding chef.

I picked up an apple pie, a cheesecake, and cupcakes from Zabar's, a gourmet specialty food store on the Upper West Side. I'm taking them with me. After dessert, we will exchange gifts. I've got a fire engine for Paul James, Mom and Mr. Robby's son, who is almost three years old. I've got a watch for Mom, a dark blue tie for Mr. Robby, and an oil paint set for Timothy.

The walls of Timothy's bedroom are covered with his artwork. He has come a long way. He's in high school and he has made friends. He stopped attending speech therapy about a year ago, and he ceased going to counseling this past summer.

I was discharged from the hospital in September 1965. I decided to delay going to college for a while. Timothy started weekend visits, and he was eventually released from foster care and came to live with Cleo and me. I took him to school and his speech and counseling appointments. We did go shopping. We also visited the Museum of Natural History frequently, and we even went ice skating in Central Park.

Cleo and Michael left for Europe right after Mom and Mr.

Robby's small and elegant wedding in December 1965. And Timothy went to live with them in Mount Vernon.

My apartment is sunny. The view of Central Park is serene, and I write. I didn't take the assistant manager job at the supermarket. I didn't need to. "My Self Face," "Miss Michaels," and "Inside Toilet" were published. An agent contacted me, and I got a pretty good advance for my Furious Red novel. It was published in the spring of 1966 and received good reviews in the *New York Times Book Review, Essence,* and the *New York Amsterdam News.* I've completed a sequel that's scheduled to be published in the spring.

Lola took the job at John Hopkins. She worked as a practical nurse and started attending school too. She's now a registered nurse. She lives in the suburbs and drives a Mustang. Last spring, she moved Aunt Rosa out of the projects and in with her. We speak occasionally but we both know we have moved on.

Charles, Cool, and his boys are all in prison. Timothy and I were spared the ordeal of testifying.

Cleo and Michael send me cards from far-off places, including Italy, Amsterdam, Paris, Greece, and Germany. They tell me that, with things the way they are (the strife in America, James Meredith shot in Mississippi, Martin Luther King assassinated in Memphis, and Bobby Kennedy killed in Los Angeles), they would not return to the United States anytime soon.

Strolling down Madison Avenue one day last year, I ran into MaryAlice, her portfolio tucked under her arm. She coughed, stammered, and tried to explain what had happened so long ago, the abortion and all, but I silenced her with a kiss.

Earl Ernest passed the bar exam and is now working at a community organization that offers legal services to people of marginal income. I have him as a good friend, along with writers I'd met here and there. I invite them over now and then. I also invite Mary Alice, Jay and Rita Ann. Jay and Rita Ann got married and moved to Jersey City, right across the George Washington Bridge. They are very close to the Upper West Side.

Miss Hazel reconciled with Rita Ann's father and moved out of the projects.

I've saved money, and I have a passport. I sometimes think about joining Cleo and Michael, but, for now, I'm staying put and writing.